ANNO DOMINI

ANNO DOMINI

three stories
by
GEORGE STEINER

The Overlook Press
Woodstock, New York

for
STORM JAMESON

Overlook Edition first published in 1980 by
The Overlook Press
Lewis Hollow Road
Woodstock, New York 12498
Copyright © 1964 by George Steiner

Library of Congress Cataloging in Publication Data
Steiner, George, 1929-
Anno Domini.

I. Title.
PZ4.S822An 1980 {PR6069.T417} 823'.914 80-15345
ISBN 0-87951-113-3

Printed in U.S.A.

TB 11/24/80

Contents

Return No More

1

He paused by the edge of the road until the truck had curved out of sight and the rasp of the motor had died in the cold salt air.

Then he shifted his rubber-tipped cane to his right hand and stooped down with the left to pick up his suitcase, torn at the hinges and lashed with string.

He advanced in spasms down the gravelled side road to the village. His right leg was dead to the hip and swung on the socket of his straining body in a slow arc. The foot, shod in a blunt shoe and raised on a bulky leather heel, slid gratingly with each step. Whereupon the man would again thrust cane and body forward and draw the leg after him.

The twist of effort had hunched his neck and shoulders as if he wore armour, and at every lunge sweat shone at the edge of his fine, reddish hair. Pain and the constant observance of precarious footing fogged his eyes to an uncertain grey. But when he gathered breath, setting his suitcase on the ground and stilting on his cane like a long-legged heron, his eyes resumed their natural colour, a deep harsh blue. The port of his head, with its fine-drawn mouth and delicate bone structure, mocked the gnarled contortion of his gait. The man was handsome in a worn, arresting way.

Ordinarily, trucks did not stop in the highroad but churned by between the dunes and the cliffline, either inland to Rouen, or farther along the coast to Le Havre. Yvebecques lay off the road, on the escarpment of the cliffs and along a half-moon of stone beach. High yellow buses stopped on their way from Honfleur, turning into the market-place. They unloaded under the wide-flung eaves of the Norman market hall. Beyond its pillared arcade ran a street, narrow and high-gabled, and at the end of it the beach, merging into the wavering light of the sea.

On the market-place stood a three-spouted brass fountain. It bore a scroll filled with names and garlanded with ceremonious laurel. Each spout curved like a desolate gargoyle over a date, heavily incised: 1870, 1914, 1939, *pro domo*.

Hearing the truck stop and shift gears, the men who stood among the market stalls or by the fountain looked up. A coldness and stiffness came over their easy stance. The fishmonger, who was hosing down his marbled stall, let the water race unchecked across his boots.

The traveller was now very near. Once again he rested his suitcase and straightened his back, letting the strain ebb from his shoulders. At the verge of the market-place, where the gravel turns to cobblestones, he paused and looked about. His mouth softened into a smile. He had not heard the brusque silence and made for the fountain. He hastened his step by sheer bent of will.

He brought his face under the live spout. The chill, rusty water spilled over his mouth and throat. Then he pushed himself upwards, pivoting adroitly on his good leg. He limped towards the red-and-yellow awning of the café. But a mass of long, unmoving shadows fell across his way. Three of the men wore the heavy smocks of fishermen; one was round, close-cropped and in a dark suit. The fifth was scarcely more than a boy. He hovered near the edge of the group and chewed his wet lip.

The stranger looked at them with a grave, hesitant courtesy, as if he had known they would be there to bar his way but had hoped for some twist of grace. The round dark one surged forward. He set his lacquered shoe against the man's cane and thrust his face close. He spoke low, but such was the stillness of the square that his words carried, distinct and raging: "No. No. Not here. Get out. We don't want you back. Any of you. Now get out."

And the boy cried, "No," in a thin, angry whine.

12

The traveller bent a little to one side, as in a sudden rouse of wind. Close by a voice flat with rage said again: "Get out. We don't want any part of you. Lucky for you you're a cripple. Not enough meat for a man on your carcass."

He squinted against the high sun and remembered his bearings. He veered from the bristling shadows and started towards the street which led from the market square to the apple orchards on the western terrace of the cliffs. But even before he had entered the dark of the Rue de la Poissonière, the boy had leaped past. He whirled, grinning with spite: "I know where you are going. I will tell them. They'll stone you alive." He spurted on and turned once more: "Why don't you catch me, cripple?"

Tight-buttoned, the notary peered after the stranger. Then he spat between his lacquered toes and whistled. A large dog rose from under the meat stalls and ambled over. A leathery cur backed mournfully from a pile of fishgut oozing on the warm stones. Other dogs came off their haunches. The notary scratched his mongrel behind the ears and hissed at it, pointing towards the limping man. Then he flicked the dog across its snout with a lash of the wrist. The animal sprang away snarling. Monsieur Lurôt hissed again and the dog understood. He fanged the fleas from his raw neck and gave a queer yelp, cruel and lost. A retriever, who had been drowsing under the billiard table, tore out of the café. Now other men were flailing and whistling at the dogs and pointing to the Rue de la Poissonière. The pack milled at the fountain snapping at each other, then hurtled towards the narrow street. In the van, Lurôt's mongrel let out a full-throated cry.

He heard them coming in a loud rush but they were at his heels before he could turn. They flew at him like crazed shadows, slobbering and snapping the air with woken fury. The man swayed off balance as he swung his cane at the bellowing pack. He was able to stem his legs against a wall but the mongrel sprang at him, its eyes flaring with vacant malignity. The rancid scent of the dog enveloped him. He flung the animal from his face but felt a hot scratch raking his shoulder.

Beyond the reek and clamour of the charging dogs, like distant streamers on the wind, the lame man heard laughter from the market-place.

The animals were wearying of their sport. They stood off, baring their teeth. Only the retriever was still at him, circling and darting in, its head low. It evaded the man's cane with jagged leaps. Suddenly the bitch hurled herself at the stranger's inert leg. Her teeth locked on the leather heel. The man went down against the side of the house, clawing the air for support. The dog inched back, its tongue red over its bruised mouth. The cane snapped down on it with a single, murderous stroke. The animal subsided into a moaning heap; somewhere a bone had cracked and now its eyes spun.

The suitcase had fallen on the cobblestones. One of the hinges sprung and a small parcel tumbled out. It had shattered against the sharp rim of the pavement. Slivers of blue and ice-white china lay dispersed in the gutter. In the murky street they gathered points of light. The man dragged himself over and picked up what was left of the Meissen figurine. Only the base, with its frieze of pale cornflowers, and the slim, silk-hosed legs of the shepherd dancer were intact. Bereft of the arching body and dreaming visage, these legs, in their plum breeches and black pumps, retained the motion of the dance. The head had smashed into myriad pieces; only the hat could be made out, lying near the middle of the street, three-cornered and with a flash of plume.

The traveller lurched to his feet, picked up his suitcase and tightened the string over the broken corner. The dogs stood wary. Then the mongrel shuffled near and whined softly. The man passed his hand over its mangy ears. Lurôt's dog looked up with a wide, stupid stare. The pack did not follow the cripple as he moved away.

Before him the houses thinned out and the cliff towered into

14

full view. The sea lay to the right, murmurous and hazy under the white sun. The salt wind dried the sweat from the man's face and body. But the yelp of the dogs had bitten into his marrow, and dim shocks of fear and tiredness passed through his limbs. In the sudden shade of the apple trees his skin prickled with cold. Now the path lifted again and the sea opened beneath him, glittering in the heat. Only the tideline moved, lapping the beach with a sullen vague rustle.

The way dipped into a hollow. Bees sang between the stubble and the grass had the dry savour of inland. Recollection came upon him vivid and exact. *Quis viridi fontes induceret umbra*—who shall veil the spring with shadow and leaf?

It was at this spot that the Latin tag had risen out of a schoolboy's harried forgetting. And its music had held through the mad clamour. He had hobbled his dawn round of the fortifications on the rim of the cliffs, inspecting the bunkers sunk into live rock, and peering through the range-finder at the still haze on the Channel. He was returning to his quarters at the farm of La Hurlette. The path was staked between minefields, and high in the booming air he could hear planes moving down the valley of the Seine on their daily, mounting runs. Far away, on the river bluffs above Rouen, anti-aircraft guns were firing short bursts. The detonations thudded as from a distant quarry.

As he had limped into the dell, all sounds had receded. He had sat down to still the rack of his body. His wound was new, and he had suffered hideously in the field hospital near Kharkhov and on the trains that wormed across Europe, furtively, with jolting detours over railbeds and bridges twisted by bombs. He had lain on a siding at the approaches to Breslau watching a bottle of morphine teeter on the shelf out of reach of his fingers. The orderlies were cowering in a ditch.

He had learned to live with his pain as one lives with a familiar yet treacherous animal. He conceived of it as a large cat which honed its claws, drawing them like slow fire from shoulder to heel, and then crouching down again in the dim and middle of his body. He had been posted to the Yvebecques sector of the Channel wall as chief of military intelligence. It was a soft billet accorded in deference to his infirmity. As the pain slunk back to its lair, that line of Virgil had sung in his bruised thoughts. With it the gate of memory swung open and behind it drowsed the rust-green gables and slow canals of the north country.

Later that year the Channel haze had reddened into savage tumult. But through the hell that ensued, he carried the verse with him, and the image of this place, a hand cupped full of silence and water, guarded from the wind.

As he came out of the hollow, still grasping his suitcase, Falk's eyes lit. La Hurlette lay just beyond the next fold in the down, where the cliff subsided under green ridges and the valley of the Coutance opened out. He could see the stream, quick and chalk-pale between marsh grass. Now the farm was in sight and recognition beat at him like a wing stroke.

The pockmarks made by mortar shells were still visible under the eaves, but rounded by time, as if clams had dug their delicate houses in the stone. The byre shone with a new red roof but the outbuildings and the clumps of lilac and holly were exactly as he had last seen them, hurtling by in a motor-cycle side-car, under wild, acid smoke, five summers ago.

Then he saw the ash tree to the left of the house and his spirit went molten. It stood in leaf, more grey now than silver. Through the foliage he could make out, unmistakable, the stab of the branch on which they had hanged Jean Terrenoire. The night the invasion had begun on the beaches to the west, a patrol had caught the boy perched near the summit of the cliff. He was signalling to the shadows at sea. They had carried him back to La Hurlette, his face beaten livid with their rifle butts. Falk sought to question him but he merely spat out his teeth. So they let the family out of the cellar for a moment to say good-bye and then dragged him to the ash tree. Falk had seen the thing done.

16

The tree had thickened but the branch retained its dragon motion and Falk could not take his eyes from it. As he started towards the house, he remembered suddenly that the Terrenoires would be waiting. The boy from the market-place had scurried before him to give warning. They would be at his throat before he could cross the threshold. Hatred lay across his path like an unsteady glare. Forcing back his shoulders, Falk glanced at the window of the corner room, his room, and saw the foxglove on the sill, as he had left it. Here had been his island in the ravening sea, here she had brought him the warm, grass-scented milk in a blue pitcher. He pressed on.

The door was loose on the latch and Falk stopped, nakedly afraid. He was momentarily blinded by the dark of the house but knew almost at once that nothing had been altered. The pots and warming-pans glowed on the wall like cuirasses of a ghostly troop. An odour of wax cloth and mouldering cheese hung over the room, and its subtle bite had stayed in his nostrils. The clock which he had bought during his convalescence in Dresden and which the Terrenoires had accepted when first he came, with neither thanks nor refusal, hammered softly on the mantelpiece.

Then he saw Blaise. He stood by the wall and in his fist Falk glimpsed the black fire iron. Blaise stared at him, his tight mouth wrenched with hatred and disbelief: "Mother of God! The half-wit wasn't lying. It *is* you. You've dared come back. You've dared crawl out here. You stinking, murdering pile of shit!" He swayed nearer: "So you've come back. *Ordure! Salaud!*" The mind's excrement of hate poured out of Blaise. He gasped for air as if rage held him by the windpipe. "I'm going to kill you. You know that, don't you? I'm going to kill you."

He reared back, his eyes crazy and hot, and lifted the iron. But old Terrenoire flung a chair at him, across the floor of the kitchen: "Stop it! *Merde.* Who do you think runs this house?" He had gone grey and sere; age had sanded down his beak nose. But the old, cunning mastery was still there, and Blaise winced as if the whip had caught him on the mouth. "No one's going to do any killing around here unless I tell them to. Remember what I said. Don't drive the fox away if you want his pelt. Perhaps Monsieur Falk has something to say to us." He looked at his guest with heavy, watchful scorn.

A low wail broke from Blaise's clenched throat: "I don't care what he says. I'll flay the hide off the stinking swine." He crouched near the fireplace like a numbed adder, venomous but unmoving.

As Falk limped towards the bench in the opaque terror of a slow, familiar dream, he saw the woman and the two girls. Madame Terrenoire's ears stood out from beneath grey, wiry hair. There were tufts of white above her eyes. Nicole had kept her straight carriage but a spinsterish tautness lay about her thin neck. Falk saw that her hands were trembling.

Danielle had turned her back. Falk bore her image with him, inviolate and precise. But it was that of a twelve-year-old. She had large grey eyes and her hair shed the heavy light of hammered gold. She had not been beautiful, having her father's nose and angular shoulders. But she possessed a darting grace of life. They spoke together often, in a hushed, courtly manner. She brought him breakfast and stole to the corner of the room to watch his orderly wax his boots and mounted heel. She did not sit by him, but stood grave and malicious, as little girls do in front of old, broken men. Every morning Falk took coffee beans and a spoonful of sugar from his rations and set them at the rim of his tray. He knew she would carry these spoils of love to her father, racing noiselessly down the stairs.

On the day of the invasion, against the whine and roar of coastal batteries, Danielle had slipped into his room. Falk was putting on his helmet and greatcoat before going to the command car camouflaged under the oak trees a thousand yards from the house. She watched him warily, the floorboards shaking to the sound of the guns. As he turned to go, easing the strap of the automatic pistol over his shoulder, she touched his sleeve with a furtive, sensuous motion. Before he could say anything she was gone, and he heard the cellar door slam heavily behind her quick steps.

He had seen her once more that night. Through his torn lips Jean Terrenoire said nothing to his family. He merely embraced each in turn while the corporal knotted the rope. Coming to Danielle, Jean knelt down and stroked her cheek. She shivered wildly in his grasp. They hurried him into the garden. As Falk passed, the girl shrank from him and made a low, inhuman sound. It had stuck in his mind like a festering thorn. Now he hardly dared look at her. But he knew at a glance that she had grown tall and that her hair still burned like autumn.

Falk sagged to the low bench. He laid the cane on the floor, under the crook of his dead leg.

"You are right. There is something I want to say to you." He looked at Blaise, coiled near him, murderous. "I pray God you will give me the time."

A black stillness was in the room. "When I left you, I had orders to reach Cuverville and re-establish Brigade headquarters. But at daylight American fighters strafed us. They came in so close to the ground that haystacks scattered under their wings. On the second pass they got Bültner, my orderly. You remember Bültner. He was a fat man and ate the green apples where they fell in the orchard. I think he was secretly in love with you, Nicole. Anyway, he was so badly hit that we dared not move him, but left him under the hedgerow propped on a blanket. I hoped the ambulance would find him in time. But some of your people got to him first. Later on we heard that they beat him to death with threshing flails.

"We could not stay in Cuverville and were dispatched to Rouen. I remember the two spires in the red smoke. An hour after we arrived, paratroopers came down in the middle of the city. Each day was the same; we moved east and there were fewer of us. In good weather the planes were at us incessantly, like a pack of wolves. We had respite only when the clouds came low. I grew to hate the sun as if it had the face of death.

"Each man has his own private surrender. At some point he knows inside himself that he is beaten. I knew when I saw what was left of Aachen. But we kept the knowledge from each other as if it was a secret malady. And we fought on. During our counter-attack in the winter I was in sight of Strasbourg. The next day my wound ripped open again. I was no further use to anyone and they shipped me back to a convalescent home, somewhere near Bonn, in a patch of wood. The windows had been blown to bits and we tacked army blankets across the frames to keep out the snow. We sat in that false dark hearing the big guns get closer. Then we heard tank treads on the road. That day the medical staff and the nurses vanished. The old doctor stayed. He said he was tired of running: had run all the way to Moscow and back. He had a bottle of brandy in front of him and would wait. He gave me my discharge papers. Some of our infantry set up a mortar in the courtyard of the house and the Americans had to use flame-throwers to get them out. I do not know what happened to the old man."

Falk shifted his weight. The sun was moving west and the light slid across the window like a long red fox.

"I had to get to Hamburg. I wanted to see my home. There had been rumours about the fire raids and I was anxious. I hardly remember how I managed to get on to a train, one of the last travelling north from Berlin. I had grown up in Hamburg and knew it like the lineaments of my own hand. What I saw when I crawled across the rubble of the station yard was unimaginable, but also terribly familiar. When I was a small boy, the teacher had tacked a greatly enlarged photograph of the moon on our classroom wall. I used to stare at it interminably, and the craters, striations and seas of dead ash were fixed in my brain. Now they lay before me. The whole city was on fire. There was no sunlight, no sky, only swirls of grey air, so hot it burned one's lips. The houses had settled into vast craters. They burned day and night homing the planes to their target.

20

But there were no more targets; only a sea of flame spreading windward with each successive raid. And wherever the ruins grew hottest, gusts of air rushed in, poisonous with stench and ash.

"I must have started yelling or running about, for a shadow came at me out of the smoke and shook me hard. It was a one-armed man in a dented helmet. He told me to get down to a shelter before the next wave passed over. The sirens were wailing again but I could barely hear them above the noise of the flames. I did not know until then that fire makes that sound—a queer hideous scratching, as if blood were seething in one's throat. The man pulled me by the sleeve; he was a warden in the police auxiliary; I was to obey him; he couldn't waste his time looking after damn fools who didn't take shelter.

"We scuttled down into a trench lined with sandbags and sheets of corrugated iron. It was full of smoke and rancid smells. I made out grey splotches in the dark. They were human faces. At first I thought they were wearing gas masks or goggles. But it was simply that they were black with soot and that the near flames had left livid streaks on their skin. Only their eyes were alive; they closed suddenly when the bombs fell. There was a small girl crouching near the open end of the trench. She was barefoot and had burn marks on her arms. She asked me for a cigarette, saying she was hungry. I had none but gave her a wafer of Dutch chocolate wrapped in silver foil. She broke it in two, thrusting one piece in her pocket and placing the other in her mouth. She sucked at it cautiously. It was still on her tongue when the all-clear sounded. She heard it before any of us, raced up the steps and disappeared into the stinging smoke. As I clambered from the trench, I saw her running beside a burning wall. She turned back and waved.

"I asked the warden how I might get to the Geiringerstrasse. He gave me a frightened, angry look. 'Isn't that where the gas tanks are?' I remembered the two grimy tanks and the wire fence around them at the upper end of the street where the foundry works began. 'The tanks are near there, yes.' 'That's what I thought. No use your going. It's all sealed off. The *Amis* have been after those gas tanks with incendiaries. They got them two days ago. No one has been allowed near the Geiringerstrasse since. Come along. We'll have a look at your papers and find you a shelter to sleep in.' But I shook him loose and hastened for home.

"New fires had driven the smoke upwards and guided me like wildly swinging lamps. In the burning craters single houses or parts of houses still stood upright. The passage of flame had traced strange designs on the walls, as if a black ivy had sprung up. Often I had to step across the dead. Some had been burned alive trapped by curtains of fire; others had been blown to pieces or struck by shrapnel. But many lay outwardly unhurt, their mouths wide open. They had died of suffocation when the flames drank the air. I saw a young boy who must have died actually breathing fire; it had singed his mouth and leaped down his throat, blackening the flesh. Scorched into the asphalt next to him was the brown shadow of a cat.

"As I drew near what had been the Löwenplatz and the beginning of the Geiringerstrasse, a cordon of men barred my way. They were Gestapo and police. They had guns and were letting no one pass. Behind them the fires burned white with a fantastic glitter. Even here, at the end of the street, the heat and stench of gas were unbearable. The heat flogged one across the eyes and nose with nauseating strokes. I felt vomit in my mouth and grew hysterical. I pleaded with one of the Gestapo officers. I must get through. My family might be trapped in there. He shook his head and whispered at me; he was too tired to speak; he had had no sleep since three nights; since the gas tanks went up. No one was allowed through. His men were in there now seeing what could be done. At that moment I heard shots being fired somewhere in the street, behind the wall of flame. I began yelling and trying to wrestle my way through the cordon. One of the policemen took me by the collar: 'Don't be an idiot.

There's nothing more we can do. We've tried everything. We're putting them out of their misery. They're begging for a bullet.' And now the burning wind brought voices, high-pitched, mad voices. The line of policemen flinched. Two Gestapo men shuffled out of the smoke and tore off their masks. They carried guns. One of them went over to a pile of rubble and fainted. The other stood in front of the officer swaying like a drunk: 'I can't go on with it, Herr Gruppenführer, I can't.' He shambled away in a sleepwalker's gait, dropping his gun. The officer turned to me with an odd look. 'You say you have some of your people in there? All right. Take that pistol and come with me. Perhaps you *can* help.' His eyes were like two red embers; there was no life in them, only smoke and fear. We put on masks and hunched through the searing wind. The Geiringerstrasse runs alongside a small canal. It was always full of oil and slag. As a boy I used to watch the sunlight break on the oil in blues and bright greens. Now, crawling forward under the blaze of the gas tanks, I saw the canal again. There were human beings in it, standing immersed up to their necks. They saw us coming and began waving their arms. But instantly they plunged their arms back into the water, screaming. The Gestapo officer lifted a corner of his mask and rasped at me: 'Phosphorus.' The Americans had dropped incendiaries made of phosphorus. Where it is in contact with air phosphorus burns unquenchably. Their clothes and bodies on fire, the people of the Geiringerstrasse had died like living torches. But a few had managed to leap into the canal. There they stood for three days. Every time they tried to crawl out of the water their clothing flared up in a yellow flame. In the heart of the fire they were dying of cold and hunger. While the freezing water slid over them, their bodies shook with burns and mad spasms. Most had given up and gone under. But a few were still erect, yelling hoarsely for food and help. The Red Cross had fed them from the banks and put blankets around their heads. But on the third day, as the raids started again, everyone had been ordered out. Nothing

could be done except to make death quicker and stop the inhuman screaming. So the Gestapo went in. Most of the faces
were unrecognizable. Hair and eyebrows had been seared away.
On the black water I saw a row of living skulls. The Gestapo
officer had drawn his pistol and I heard him firing. One of the
faces was staring at me. It was a girl, and on her scorched
forehead the flames had left a tuft of hair, red like mine. Her
lips were baked and swollen but she was trying to form words.
I crept over to her and took off my mask. The heat and reek of
phosphorus made me gag. But I was able to lean out over the
canal and she drifted towards me, her eyes never leaving mine.
Her tongue was a charred stump but I understood what she was
saying. 'Quickly. Please. Quickly.' I slipped my arm behind her
head and put my lips to hers. She leaned back and closed her
eyes. Then I shot her. I can't be sure. The faces were too far
gone. Yet I am sure it was my sister."

The room was still as winter. In the gathered shadows the
chime of the clock had grown remote and unreal. Suddenly
Danielle spoke, without turning around, loud into the dark air:
"Good. Good. I am glad."

Her voice sprang at Falk out of an ambush long dreaded but
now intolerable. The hatred of it stunned him. It seemed to
close over his head in a suffocating tide. The pain that had been
lurking in his bent, immobile leg surged to a shrill pitch. It shot
into his back and set his neck in a vice. The drag and harshness
of the long day racked his will. Only the pain was real, like a
red fist before his eyes, and it beat towards the ground. But
even at the instant where something inside him, something of
the quick of hope and bearing, was about to break, Danielle
rose and moved swiftly past him. Her hand brushed against his
sleeve in dim remembrance.

Falk raised his head to look after her and the pain grew bearable, ebbing into his hips, where it gnawed in sharp but familiar
guise. Terrenoire got up and lit the lamp on the sideboard. It
threw the shadow of his hooked nose against the wall like a

child's drawing of a pirate. Madame Terrenoire and Nicole cleared the dishes, stacking the white and blue china. They did not look at the crippled man on the bench.

Blaise came off his haunches, his cat's eyes livid. He spat at Falk's clubfoot with derisive loathing and swore under his breath: "*Nom de Dieu.*" Then he picked up the milk pail in an easy motion and went out the door. Before it swung close, Falk caught a glimpse of the early stars.

He woke with a numb jolt. The sourness of broken sleep lay thick on his tongue. Momentarily he did not know where he was. Night was in the room and the events of the past few hours passed vaguely through his thoughts. Then he saw a shadow looming at him out of the stairwell. On guard, Falk groped for his cane. His fingers tightened on the grip, but nearly at once he recognized a familiar patch of white lace; Madame Terrenoire's nightcap, and beneath it the flat, coarse features of the ageing woman. She rustled towards him in her frayed houserobe, leaned against the stove and searched him out with her shallow eyes. Her scrutiny slid over him like a blind man's hand, neutral yet inquisitive.

Then she asked abruptly: "Why have you come back here? Was it to tell us that vile story . . . *cette sale histoire*?"

"Yes," said Falk.

"Is the story true?"

"Yes," he said again, beyond outrage.

"You are lying," she said, not in anger, but with malignity. "You are lying. You didn't come back here just to tell us what happened to you. Why should we care? You've come back to take something from us. I know your kind. That's all you're good for. To take and take and take." The hands in her lap opened and closed rapaciously.

"You have so much to give," said Falk.

She arched like an old cat: "Not any more. You've taken it all. You took Jean and hanged him on that cursed tree. You

25

took so many of our young men that Nicole has been left a spinster. Just look at her. She'll soon be dry wood. Blaise is a ruffian. He was never meant to be an oldest son. When you killed Jean there was no one else for us to lean on. It's made him a brute. And what about me? I'm an old woman. There's hardly anyone left around here except the children and the old. You took the rest and hanged them on the trees. No, there's nothing more to take." She closed her mouth hard, and to Falk she seemed like an astute fish snapping for air and then diving back into silence.

"Perhaps it's my turn to give. Giving and taking . . . *c'est parfois la même chose*. It's sometimes the same act." She brushed the thought aside with a contemptuous flutter of her hand.

But Falk persisted: "It was easy to take. Too easy. We must learn to receive from each other." She gave no sign of comprehension. "It may be that you are right, that I have come to take again. But what I can take from you this time is not life. It is some part of the death that lies between us. *Un peu de cette mort*."

She countered relentlessly: "I don't understand you. Taking is taking."

"Even when it is love?" Falk asked awkwardly.

She gave a dry laugh: "*Vous êtes de beaux salauds*. You're a fine lot of swine. To speak of love in a house where you've murdered a child."

"But that is exactly the house in which I must speak of it. Don't you see? After everything that's happened, where else can it have any meaning?"

Something in his vehemence stung her but she yielded no ground: "You talk like a priest, but I know you for what you are. How could I forget? You killed Jean. Out there, on that ash tree."

"None of us are what we were. Try me again."

She shrugged him off: "What for? Leave us alone. There's no place for your kind among us. We've seen you too often. You've been at our throats three times. *Ça suffit*."

She turned from him with distaste as if she had expended too richly from her small hoard of words. But at the foot of the stairs she paused and after a spell turned with a queer jerk: "That bench can't be much good for sleeping. You look as stiff as a dead mackerel. God knows why I'm letting you spend the night here." Yet even as she said it, a note of pleased cunning stole into her hacking voice: "There's a room at the top of the house, with a bed in it. I don't have to show *you* the way." Madame Terrenoire started up the wooden stairs. Falk hobbled across the kitchen. She waited for him to come near, looked back and said between her teeth: "It was Jean's bed. See whether you can sleep in it, Captain."

Having reached the musty room under the gables, Falk looked out the window and saw the moon in the orchard. Beyond the brittle noise of the crickets he caught the grating of the sea. He sat there for a long time, scarcely breathing the stale, warm air. When at last he fell back on the bedspread, the first glint of sunrise was visible on the eastern cliffs like a thread of copper in the morning grass.

The moment of pure, unthinking vengeance had passed. Werner Falk was endured at La Hurlette like one of those masterless dogs who forage at the edge of a farm. Hatred crackled under his feet in vicious spurts. Blaise was dark with outrage and the old woman looked on Falk with a patient contempt more insidious than fury. But they did not touch him when he passed in reach of the scythe or the heavy spade. The hideousness of his tale, the offering of it in exchange of grief, gave him sanctuary. Though they were only obscurely aware of it, the Terrenoires treated Falk as if there was on his skin the white shadow of leprosy.

Terrenoire himself said nothing. He observed Falk with gloomy complaisance; he discerned in his queer, unbidden arrival a hint of vantage. Nicole cast words at Falk now and again, and when they stood near each other a low flame lit in her sallow cheeks. She gazed after him when he trailed off to the steaming fields in the hot of the morning and threw him a nervous, irritated look when he returned at twilight from the cliffs. Only Danielle stayed outside the wary game. When they chanced to meet in the stairwell or across the neutral ground of the kitchen, her eyes narrowed with pain.

In the village voices rose and fell. Everyone knew that the German captain had returned to La Hurlette and that his presence there was being suffered in the very shade of the ash tree. Around Lurôt's table at the Café du Vieux Port anger and wonderment eddied. But the Terrenoires were regarded as deep ones. Drawing the pale white wine through his lips, Lurôt concluded that there was doubtless something to be reaped from Falk's visit. The Terrenoires were no fools; *ce ne sont pas des poires.* Vague, covetous suspicion hardened to belief: Falk had come to pay compensation for Jean's death. The Germans were rich now, filthy rich. What had he carried in his suitcase? Some of the banknotes and jewellery which the boches had looted from France. There would be a new thresher soon at La Hurlette.

So the villagers waited and pondered, like a herd of cattle, pawing the earth now and again in drowsy malevolence. They bore Falk's coming and going, though a sullen tremor ran under their skin as he passed. Soon they paid no heed and were hardly aware of the limping figure that emerged from the orchards to sit on the stone beach in the glitter of noon.

After three o'clock the tide receded nearly to the base of the cliff gate, leaving behind a green, shimmering expanse. Women and children swarmed out to harvest shrimp and mussels. Falk delighted in their scurrying progress and the swift fall of the nets. Often he hobbled a short distance into the unsteady ooze of stone and trapped sea.

A week after his arrival at La Hurlette he saw Nicole just ahead of him, her skirts tucked high. She turned and called under her breath: "*Venez donc.* Come on out."

28

He followed precariously. Weed-covered and smoothed by the tides, the rocks were like glass. Between them lay brackish puddles. The afternoon sun played brokenly on the water, and rock and sand flickered like a mosaic. Falk slithered to his knees in the tangle of red weeds. Nicole stayed just in front of him, flinging words over her shoulder so that he had to strain after them.

"The others are wondering why you've come back. Blaise wanted to kill you on the spot. He still does. But I won't let him." She turned for an instant, her face strangely flushed. "I told *maman* you had no other place to go. All your people in Hamburg are dead. We're the closest thing you have to a home." He caught the abrupt laugh in her voice: "It sounds mad, doesn't it? But I'm sure it's true. You were happy at La Hurlette. We knew that. I think that's why Jean hated you so much. If only you had been unhappy among us or treated us badly, we could have borne it. But to see you come through the door in your grey coat as if it was really home to you, as if you were at peace, that was unendurable. You were terribly good-looking then. Do you know that? It made it worse."

Falk slid grotesquely into a trough of bubbling sand but her arm swung back and held him. They stood beside each other on a rock at the edge of the flats. Before them the sea heaved in a drowsy swell. All around the herring gulls yawped and scoured for their prey. Nicole lifted her chin into the wind: "We were all afraid of you. We had to be. But Jean hated you. Perhaps because he admired you so much; for being an officer and for the books you brought with you. He used to steal up to your room and read them while you were away. I wonder whether you knew." Falk did not answer but bent close to catch her words amid the hiss of the returning sea. "He tried to read the books of German poetry. And the thick one in the yellow wrapper. It was by a philosopher, wasn't it? With a long name. I don't remember. It drove Jean crazy to think you could have such books and treasure them. He wanted to kill you. It wouldn't have been so difficult either. The way you used to come down alone from the cliff at nightfall. But they wouldn't let him."

"They?"

"The cell he belonged to, the *réseau* he took orders from in Le Havre. They didn't believe in acts of individual terrorism. Or so they claimed."

"Who were they?"

"Surely you knew. Jean was in the Party."

She faced him, her mouth drawn thin. "He was a rabid communist. We thought you had found out. That's why you hanged him, wasn't it?"

Falk shook his head and tried to keep his footing on the wet rock: "No, we had no knowledge of that. We hanged your brother because he was signalling to the Canadian landing barges from the top of the cliff."

"Ah. Was that the only reason? *Qu-importe?* He wanted to kill you and you killed him instead. That's war, isn't it?" She said it with indifference, as if it was a truth long buried. "Father had no love for Jean. They fought like dogs. When he discovered that Jean was going around with communists, he beat him half to death. But Jean grew to be stronger than *papa*. He didn't dare lay a hand on him later on. So they snarled at each other continually."

"What about you, Nicole? Did you get on with Jean?"

"No," she said. "I'm not a hypocrite like the others. So I'll tell you. We never cared much for each other. I was the oldest but he showed me no regard. With his books and glib talk and stupid politics, you would have thought he was some kind of genius. But he wasn't. I'd say he was an arrogant puppy and that's the truth. No, there was no love lost between us. He knew I was plain-looking and used to joke about it with the other louts in the village. Said I was tall and bony as an old rake; that's what they whispered behind my back, *vieux râteau*. After you came I suddenly realized that Jean was nothing but a little boy, a clever little boy playing at war. I told him how good-looking you were and that you were a real soldier. It made him livid." Nicole glanced away in vexed remembrance. "When you killed him, I knew that I should feel bitter grief. But I felt nothing. Nothing at all. Danielle howled for days. We couldn't get her to eat or take her dirty clothes off. She adored Jean. She was the only one of us to whom he was gentle and they had all sorts of secrets. But I felt nothing. When the invasion came that morning, I had only one thought: perhaps I shall survive, perhaps there is going to be an end to this terrible time."

"So that's why you've forgiven me," said Falk.

"Forgiven? *Il n'est pas question de ça.* I'm no priest. I'm not interested in the past. I wish the past had never been. We must start living again. What have we to do with the dead? That's why you've come back, isn't it? You've come back to La Hurlette to show that the past need not matter, that we can salvage from it what was good and leave the rest behind like a bad dream, haven't you?" She flung the question at him with a sudden imperious surge, as if opening to the wind a hidden banner. Falk was startled by the intensity of life in her sharp features.

She bore in on him: "That's what I've told them at home. Let him be. He's going to stay with us and make good for the past. Blaise and *papa* think you're going to pay them or make some kind of cosy deal. The fools. They must think you sell cider in Germany!" Her gaiety stung. "But let them think that. It will give us time." Her hand touched his in fierce, shy demand. Falk saw the waters rising and said nothing.

Nicole lashed out at his silence: "Why don't you say something?" Her lips whitened and she drew nearer to him. "Why don't you look me in the face?"

Her nakedness appalled him. He spoke her name softly and in fear, as if it was an open wound: "Nicole. You've understood many things which I've felt. You've said the things for which I found no right words. But I don't think there can be between

31

us . . ." He stared at the moving sand, "I don't think you and I, however close we must be to one another. . . ."

Their faces were only inches apart. "You don't think that you and I. . . ." Nicole stared at him bewildered. "Not you and I. . . . Why then have you come back?" Falk reached towards her but she flinched away. "What are you doing here? What kind of a foul trick are you playing on us?"

"I know," said Falk, "it doesn't make sense. I am like a sleepwalker looking for that which kept me alive in the daytime. Looking for the one door that opens out of night. Probably I shan't be allowed anywhere near it. It's madness, I know. But you will understand, Nicole. You must understand."

She had already begun moving away. Her face had gone ashen. Only her eyes were alive and brimming with pain. Falk had once seen a gunner whip a horse across the eyes and he remembered the glare of anguish.

"Listen to me, Nicole, I beg you. I need your help. I need to know that you do not hate me. Without you I shall be hounded away from here. Just listen to me for a moment. Please."

He called in vain. The girl was racing back towards the beach, skipping with grim agility from rock to rock. She glanced back at him only once, but across the gap of wind and spray he could see the fury in her. When he looked up again, he realized he was alone. The other fishermen were hastening landward. Over the entire flats and in the dark pools the water was seething in annunciation of the returning tide. The gulls were veering towards their nests in the high cliff and the sun glowed red on their wings. Falk saw that the sea was close upon him. He clambered towards the shore. But the tide was quicker. It sent sheets of foam flashing past him and the rocks grew vague under the charge and retreat of the surf. Crabs rose warily out of the quaking mud and scuttled away from his groping steps. He fell and slithered and drew himself up again, but the water sucked at his weight. Despite the chill wind, he was drenched with sweat. Soon his hands, grasping their way along the rock edges, were raw and torn. The salt bit into his broken nails. In the failing light the beach grew distant and the roofs took on a remote, mocking blue. Labouring against the undertow, Falk remembered an ugly moment south of Smolensk. In pursuit of the Russians, his company had tumbled into a marsh. Unable to keep rank in the knife-edged grass, sickened by the flies and the stench of dead water, he and his men had crawled forward on their bellies, looking for steady ground. The enemy had turned on them with mortar fire. Wherever the shells dropped, stinking water sprayed over the wounded and the dead. Clawing his way through the lashing surf, his hands bloodied, Falk remembered the episode. The knowledge that he had got out alive screwed his will to a last, fierce effort. He lunged out of the flailing tide and on to the pebbles. On hands and knees he drew himself to a pile of nets drying in the late sun and looked back. The sea was yelping at the shore like a pack of foxes; its cold tongue darted at him still.

Nicole had raced blindly through the orchards. She met Danielle on the stairs and said in a strangled voice: "It's you he's after. It's you. Make the best of it, *petite garçe.*" Danielle stared at her in bewildered protest and raised her hand as if to ward off a blow. But all she felt were Nicole's fingers brushing her forehead as if in dubious benediction.

The next morning Terrenoire broke his silence. Falk had watched him feeding a sow as she hammered her pink snout against the trough. Closing the wire fence behind him, Terrenoire asked, "How long are you planning to stay with us, Monsieur Falk?" And before Falk could reply: "Not that it bothers me. It's no skin off my back. I told Clotilde you would be paying for your room and board, and paying better than last time. But you seem to be stirring up the girls, just like you did when you first came. They're running about like crazy hens. *Et parbleu,* you must admit it's a strange place for you to choose for a holiday."

"I'm not here for a holiday," said Falk; "it's more serious than that. In fact, it's the only completely serious thing I've ever tried to do."

Terrenoire blinked peevishly at the implication of obscure, private motive.

"I grew up in a kind of very loud bad dream," said Falk. "I cannot remember a time when we were not marching or shouting and when there were no flags in the street. When I think of my childhood all I can remember distinctly are the drums and the uniform I wore as a young pioneer. And the great red flags with the white circle and the black hooked cross in the middle. They were constantly draped across our window. It seems to me I always saw the sun through a red curtain. And I remember the torches. One night my father woke me suddenly and tore me to the window. The whole street was full of men marching with torches like a great fiery worm. I must have yelled with fear or sleepiness and my father slapped me across the mouth. I don't remember much about him but he smelled of leather.

"School was worse. The drums beat louder and there were more flags. On the way home we played rabbit hunt and went after Jews. We made them run in the gutter carrying our books and if they dropped any we held them down and pissed in their faces. In the summer we were taught how to be men. They sat us on a log two by two. Every boy in turn would slap his partner as hard as he could. First one to duck was a coward. I passed out once but did not fall off the log. I never finished school. I suppose my final exam came in Lemberg when they told me to clean out a bunker with a flame-thrower. I had my graduation in Warsaw, marching with the victory parade. Now the drums never stopped. They were always pounding at us: in Norway; outside Utrecht, where I got my first wound; in Salonika, where we hanged the partisans on meat hooks; and at Kharkov, where this happened." Falk's hand trailed absently along his leg.

"They never stopped, and in the hospital outside Dresden I thought they would drive me mad. I can't tell you much about

34

it, Monsieur Terrenoire, because I hardly remember it myself. There were two of me. One night I came hobbling down the ward back from the latrine. There was no bed vacant. I must have hopped from bed to bed looking. Then I remembered that my fever chart had a number. I found it. There was another man in my bed. I saw the stain seeping along his bandaged leg and knew that this man was I. So I jumped on him and tried to get at his throat. After that they kept me under morphine."

They had strayed into the orchard. Falk went on: "Then I was sent here. How can I explain? In church they tell us that Lazarus rose from his stinking shroud having been four days dead. And they call *that* a miracle! I had been dead twenty years. I did not really know that there was such a thing as life. No one had told me. I first stumbled on that dangerous secret here, at La Hurlette. You probably don't even remember the first night I spent with you."

Terrenoire looked at him guardedly: "I can't say I do."

Falk laughed, his voice exultant: "Why should you? It was a night like many others. Officers had been billeted here before I came. To you it meant nothing: just another unwelcome stranger in the house. But for me it was the first hour of grace. I stood up there at the window under the gables, looked across the orchard and caught a flash of the sea. Danielle—do you remember how slight and small she was?—rapped at my door and brought me a pitcher of milk. It was a blue pitcher and the milk was warm. I know these are all perfectly ordinary things, a room with a low ceiling, a row of apple trees and a blue pitcher. But to me, at that moment, they were the gates of life. *Lazare, veni foras.* But that man had been dead only four days! In this house I rose from a death much longer and worse. That night, when Danielle set the pitcher down on the table, the drums stopped beating for the first time. I never heard them here. Oh, I know the war was everywhere around us, that there were mines at the end of the garden, and barbed wire on the cliffs. But it didn't seem to matter. I saw life sitting in your

35

kitchen as if it was a brightness. Isn't that an absurd thought? But those who have grown up dead have such visions. And because the drums had stopped, I began hearing myself. I had never really heard my own voice before. Only other men's shouts and the echo we had to give. That's all I had been taught to do, echo shout for shout and hatred for hatred. It sounds fantastic, I know, but watching you and your children, I realized that human beings don't always shout at each other. The silence in this house was like fresh water, I plunged my hands and face in it. And I discovered that men are not always either one's friends or one's enemies, but somewhere in between. They had forgotten to tell us that in the *Hitlerjugend* and the *Wehrmacht*." Falk thrust his hand among the powdery blossoms. "This is where I climbed out of the grave, Monsieur Terrenoire, in your house and among these trees."

Terrenoire ground a cigarette under his mired boots: "Perhaps you did, monsieur. I don't know about such things. You say you climbed out of a grave. But, *nom de Dieu*, it didn't stay empty. You put my son in it." He glanced at Falk with a hint of satisfaction, like a player who has landed a difficult shot. He repeated the words savouring their astute propriety: "*Non monsieur*, it didn't stay empty very long, that fine grave of yours."

"I know," said Falk, "I killed your son in an act of futile reprisal, and in the hour of his victory. I found life in this house and brought death. You are right. Open graves gape until they are filled. That one should have had me in it." He said it with harsh finality, as if it was a lesson learnt long ago and implacably repeated. "I don't deny that for a moment. How could I?" Terrenoire watched from under his lids. He had seen larks fling themselves about thus before yielding to the net. "And I can't make it good to you, ever. There is no price on death."

"To be sure," said the old man, "those are the very words I used to Clotilde. He can't make up for Jean's death. They've paid the Ronquiers for the trees they sawed down, and more than they were worth, believe me. But they don't pay for the sons they killed. So I said to her: Monsieur Falk must have something else in mind." And again he blinked with an air of patient complicity.

"When I had to get out of here, the drums began all over again. I've told you what happened to me. But though I lived in hell and saw enough of horror each day to drive a man insane, it could no longer destroy me. Even at the worst, in Hamburg, after they dragged me away from the canal, and then in Leipzig when the Russians were on us, I could shut my eyes for an instant and imagine myself back at La Hurlette. I swore that if that blue pitcher went unbroken so would I. Before decamping with my men, I buried it under a mound of hay in your barn. It must be there still. I should know if anything had happened to it; something inside me would have a crack. Because I had lived here, I knew that outside the world of the mad and the dead there was something else, something that might survive the war intact. I swore I would come back one day and hear the silence."

Terrenoire plucked a wet hair from the corner of his mouth: "That's very moving, Monsieur Falk, though I don't pretend to understand all of it. *Mais c'est gentil,* and I can see that a place like this would seem better than *Wehrmacht* barracks or the Russian front. But now you've come back and had a good look. Just like the Americans who come here every summer to show their families the beaches and the cemeteries. But I don't see you packing your suitcase. On the contrary, you seem to be settling in. *À quoi bon?* What do you really want from us?"

"I wasn't sure until I came back," said Falk, "I knew inside me all the time, but didn't dare think it through. Now I know, beyond any doubt. I am in love with Danielle. I have been the whole time. I want to marry her."

Terrenoire's face opened, startled and off guard. "You want to marry Danielle?" He was fending for time, like a clam burrowing.

"If she will have me."

"If she will have you? *Parbleu,* she's not the only one con-

37

cerned. *Non, monsieur*, things are not that simple around here."
He was on his own terrain now and confident. "You've killed
my eldest son and want to marry my youngest daughter. *Drôle
d'idée.* You Germans are deep ones, I'll say that for you." He
laughed drily.

Falk made a tired, submissive gesture: "Five years are gone
since that happened. It's unredeemable, I know. But Danielle
and I are alive, and there can be children and new life
here."

"No doubt," countered Terrenoire, "but there are many
things to be thought of." Falk passed his hand over the bark of
a young tree: "You are right, Monsieur Terrenoire. I don't
even know whether Danielle will listen to me. I fear she will
laugh in my face."

"Haven't you spoken to her yet?" "No," said Falk. A glint
of malice lit in Terrenoire's pupils: "But you have spoken to
Nicole?" Falk was silent. "That was stupid of you, Monsieur
Falk. You Germans have no finesse, for all your lofty ideas."
The two men had drifted to the edge of the sown field. The
haystacks smoked slightly under the morning sun and to the
left the ash tree cast its blue shadow. "But perhaps you were
right after all," said Terrenoire: "This matter really concerns
Nicole." He cracked his knuckles: "*Dans mon pays*, monsieur,
we don't marry off our younger daughters before their older
sisters are settled. *Et voilà.*"

Both the force and the irrelevance of the argument struck
Falk. Even as he answered, pleading that there must be ex-
ceptions to such rules, his own words seemed to him feeble and
wide of the mark. Terrenoire did not bother to refute him, but
pressed forward: "Nicole will make you a good wife. She's a
little dry, *un peu sec*, like her mother, but a solid girl. She enjoys
putting her nose in books, like you do, Monsieur Falk. She
won't give you any trouble." He warmed to his theme: "You
may have got hold of something with all your fine talk. You
can't replace Jean on the farm with that leg of yours, but you

38

can make a proper home for Nicole and help us out a bit. That's some return for what we had to put up with."

Falk intruded vehemently. There could be no question of marriage between himself and Mademoiselle Nicole, though he was fond and admiring of her. He was in love with Danielle. That she was the younger sister was awkward, he granted, but it couldn't be helped. If Danielle would not have him, he would leave at once and the Terrenoires would see no further trace of him. "*Merde*," said the old man, "Danielle is much too young for you. I won't allow it. She's too young."

"I am ten years older than she is. But we're exactly the same age. We've seen and endured the same things. Outside Odessa we rounded up a group of partisans and made ready to hang them. Among them there was a Jewish boy. I couldn't believe that he was a day over fifteen. I asked him. He answered: 'I am fifteen add a thousand. To get a Jew's proper age, you should always add a thousand.' It's like that with the whole lot of us. For those who lived in the war, ten years' difference hardly matters. We carry the same mark."

Terrenoire broke off. Words were like pips in his mouth; he spat them out and was done with them. Shuffling back to the farmyard, he kept aloof from Falk's urgent plea. He stopped for a moment at the pigpen and clucked his tongue, loud as a pistol shot. The sow shifted her haunches in lazy recognition. Nearly at the threshold, Terrenoire turned bitterly: "Get one thing through your head, Monsieur Falk: if you marry Danielle, you won't get a penny out of me, *pas un liard*. I'll put her out like a beggar. With Nicole it might be different. I don't say I could give you much. You and your friends saw to that. But Nicole is the oldest. She wouldn't leave my house empty-handed."

"I don't expect anything," said Falk. "That has never entered my mind. On the contrary." Terrenoire looked up. "I have put some money aside. I am an electrical engineer. I'm partner in a small business in Hanover. We are well on our feet. On the contrary, Monsieur Terrenoire, it is I. . . ."

39

They entered the kitchen. Madame Terrenoire was scraping carrots over a cracked bowl. "You'll never guess," said Terrenoire with a watery smile, "Monsieur Falk has not come back to buy apples or see the landscape. *Il est prétendant, parbleu*; he is a suitor." She said nothing, but her hands ceased from their quick labour.

Falk found no immediate occasion to press his suit. Danielle had left for Harfleur, where her aunt kept a draper's shop. Falk remembered the little lady, hewn like a benevolent gargoyle out of a pink, brittle stone. Tante Amélie lived in implacable detestation of the English; she regarded them as cunning wolves who had sought to ruin France either by direct incursion or by entangling her in bloody wars for their own secret profit. Forced to leave her home when the old port had been turned into a German bastion, Amélie had gone to live with a bachelor cousin in Angers. She had passed through La Hurlette, giving away bales of cloth and her stock of ribbons lest they fall into English hands. She had welcomed Falk as an ally brought into France by harsh but provident destiny. When she chronicled for him the numerous occasions on which the English had sacked Harfleur, the antique conflagrations seemed to burn in her high cheeks.

Danielle often went over to Harfleur to spend a day in the musty shop, passing her fingers over the raw linen and *crépes de chine*. Nicole told Falk in a dead voice that her sister was coming home by the late afternoon bus. He went to Yvebecques to meet her.

Watching Danielle step off the bus, Falk experienced a sense of painful unreality. He had rehearsed the scene too often in his imagination, first in the prisoner-of-war camp at Dortmund, and later in Hanover when trying to salvage life out of the rubble. Now the girl came towards him as in a warm, abstract remembrance. Even the excitement that rose in him was stale. And because he was numb and momentarily remote, Falk saw

Danielle as she really was, not as he had obstinately dreamt her.

She had grown straight but her body had not filled out. It was full of hollows and awkward movement. Only her face had taken on a broad strength. The large grey eyes and steady mouth gave it an alert, nearly masculine beauty, but one could discern flat bones under the skin. Danielle would take after her mother, and Falk glimpsed, beneath the nearing girl, the later woman, secretive and perhaps a little coarse.

In an instant, however, he could no longer see her as someone apart from himself. Crossing the market-place and entering the Rue de la Poissonnière, she had passed completely into the troubled light of his desire.

Seeing Falk, Danielle gave a small, abrupt nod, as if to say, "I knew you would be here. I have been thinking about it on the bus, all the way from Harfleur"; but neither spoke. She came near and suddenly put her hand out as adversaries do before a match. Unready, Falk did not meet her gesture and their hands fumbled. At this they laughed, the strain holding them close. She began walking beside him, slowing her step to his laboured progress.

They said nothing until the road started climbing away from the village. But Falk could not keep his glance from her hair. The blood ached in his temples. When Danielle spoke, it was as if their thoughts had already conversed in intimate dispute. "Are there no girls left in Germany, Monsieur Falk?" He started. "That's what I said to Tante Amélie. Poor Monsieur Falk. There are no girls left in Germany. *Pas une seule*. So he had to pack his suitcase and come all the way to Yvebecques to find one."

"And what did your aunt say to that?"

"She told me not to worry my head about such matters but to thank *la bonne Vierge Marie* that you had come back. Tante Amélie is very taken with you, you know. You should visit her in Harfleur."

"I hope to," said Falk.

"Yes, she's still hoping that you will defeat the English. You've let her down badly."

"I'm afraid we'll have to explain to her that it didn't work out that way."

"It didn't, did it?" said Danielle lightly.

"No. But that's over and done with. It happened a long time ago."

"A long time?" she echoed him as from a far dimness.

"Yes, longer than we need remember. Believe me, Danielle."

"I thought so too. Until you walked back into our kitchen the other night. When I saw you again I heard the ash tree creaking. I had not heard it creak that way since the winter after you left. And when I ran past you I went into the garden. The bark is still worn where the rope was."

"No. That's not true. The bark has renewed itself and the branch has grown."

"That would be too simple," said Danielle.

Falk blazed up as if she had touched the very nerve of him. "Simple? On the contrary. It's much simpler to stiffen in silence or hate. Hate keeps warm. That's child's play. It would have been much simpler for me to die in Hamburg near the canal. Or to stay in Hanover and marry a widow with a pension and cast the image of you out of my mind. Do you think it's easy to come back here? In Germany we don't talk about the past. We all have amnesia or perhaps someone put an iron collar around our necks so that we can't look back. That's one way of doing it. Then there's the other, the unrelenting way. Steep yourself in the remembered horrors. Build them around you like a high safe wall. Is that any less easy or dishonest?"

She lashed out: "God knows I wish the past didn't exist! I didn't ask for those memories, did I? You forced them down our throats, the whole savage pack of you! And now you come and tell us we should forget and live for the future. You're spitting on graves. The dead will start howling when you pass."

She broke off; there were tears of rage in her voice. Had Falk

42

not grasped her arm she would have darted ahead. But he held her rooted. "Try and understand what I'm saying. I'm not asking you to forget anything. I want you to remember your brother, and, if you must, the burn of the rope on the branch. But remember Bültner also. Think of the apples he threw at you and think of him lying alive in the ditch when they came with their flails. And if you think of all the dead, of yours and of ours, it will become more bearable. I don't want you to forget. The stench of forgetting is so strong in Germany that I came back here to breathe real air. But that's only the beginning, the easy part, like learning to walk again. They taught me that in the hospital. It hurt so much I kept passing out. But it was really very simple. It's after you've learnt to walk that the terrible part begins. Suddenly you discover that you have to go some place."

"I don't want to go. I want to be left alone." And she drew away into the evening shadows.

When Falk caught up with her, lights were coming on in the village. On the horizon a tanker moved like a black thread across the molten wake of the sun. The air was still with the first touch of night.

Danielle turned to him: "Nicole is in love with you." She said it with the solemn malice of a child.

"Don't mock me."

"No. It's true. We used to quarrel about you when we were girls. We knew how handsome you were but pretended you wore a mask and vied with one another in describing how fearful you would look without it. She said she couldn't stand you because you were nasty and conceited and gave yourself airs like an old rooster. I was silly in those days and believed her. But after you left she went grey inside. She never found anyone else. When she turned down Jacques Estève—his people own the dairy on the road to Fécamp—I ran after him and told him to chop off one of his legs. He thought I was mad. If *la Sainte Vierge* has brought you back here, it's for Nicole's sake.

43

She will make you happy. *Elle sera bonne pour vous.* She's clever and serious. She knows ever so much more than I do. She can understand your books and the long words you use. And I would be your sister-in-law. Then we could sit by the chimney and talk about your children."

Involuntarily, Falk took up her tone: "And what about your children, *belle-soeur?*"

"Mine? Ah, the little horrors! Jean—he's the oldest one, you know—will always be in trouble. They'll send him home from school for putting girls' pigtails in the inkwell and for writing wicked things on the walls. So I shall have to be very angry with him. I shall pack him off to Germany to work in his uncle's factory. You will have a factory, won't you? And you will tell me how he's getting on and see to it that he writes his *maman.* And when he comes home I shall be proud of him, and he will have learned to be an engineer like you."

In the pending darkness Danielle seemed to discern the shapes of her invention. She moved after them: "And there will be many daughters. Four at least. They will have long red hair and blue eyes, not grey like mine. I shall have to go to Rouen and Le Havre to find husbands for them. They will be so pert that no one will want them."

"And what will you do then?"

"I shall send them to you and ask you to put them in a nunnery deep in the Black Forest! Tell me, is it really black?"

"Yes."

"They won't like that. They will drape their red hair out the window until someone rescues them and there will be a mighty scandal. So I shall have to bring them home and build them a house up on the *grande falaise.* There they will sit and stick their tongues out at passers-by and grow into spinsters like four tall candles."

"Will you visit them?"

"From time to time. When the wind is high. And we will gather at the fire to talk about the past."

"What will you tell them of the past?"

Danielle wavered and then bent near: "That it was long ago."

Falk found her clasped hands. He opened them gently. But beneath his soft motion she felt the surge of longing, watchful and implacable. It filled her with strange anguish, as if the entire weight of the night was upon her. She drew back rebellious: "Look," she cried out, "look!"

Falk turned heavily. Banks of clouds had mounted in the northern sky. But here and there they were thinning out; behind them shimmered a vague white line. "England," she said, "those are the English cliffs."

"I don't think so," said Falk trying to keep the edge out of his voice, "it's probably moonlight reflecting on the clouds. You rarely see the English coast from here. Even with our glasses it was difficult to tell whether we were seeing cliffs or a trick of light."

"I remember your glasses," said Danielle quickly, "in their big leather case. Do you still have them?"

"No, I sold them to an American soldier for a tin of coffee. What else do you remember?"

"Everything. The smell of your coat and the loose strap on your helmet and the way you kept forgetting your furred gloves in the kitchen. And I remember the time after you left. I tried to hate you. With every nerve inside me. I kept my eyes tight shut so that I could see before me Jean's body and the bit of rope your men left on the ash tree. But I didn't succeed. That was what made me ill. I couldn't hate you. I didn't know how." But even as she said it the weight of his presence enveloped her and she fought against it: "You see, Monsieur Falk, I am a silly girl. I don't know much about hatred and I don't know about love. *Je suis bonne à rien.*" She laughed as if she had sprung free from his reach.

"Have you never been in love, Danielle?"

"Oh, many times!"

"Seriously?"

45

The hurt in his voice provoked her: "Desperately. With Siccard at the florist's. With Monsieur Lurôt's cousin who lives in Rouen and owns two silk waistcoats. With Fridolin. He drives a green truck and takes me for rides in it."

"And now?"

The lightness drained away; something urgent and wearing rose at her. She sought to force it down. She liked to tear green currants off the bush and put them between her teeth. It was the same bitter, exciting taste. Falk asked again, "And now?"

"I don't know. I don't know."

They had not taken the straight way to La Hurlette but had strayed on to a small path which led to the rim of the cliff. There it plunged sharply down the face, ending in a niche dug out of the rock. Just large enough for two men, the hollow had served as a machine-gun nest. Looming from the dirt parapet, the barrel had a cruel sweep of the bay. Below it the cliff fell sheer into the sea. Like a gannet's eyrie, the narrow platform hung suspended between the dark folds of the rock and the clamour of the water. Falk had often gone there to inspect the watch, to inhale the salt rush of night or peer at the red flashes on the English coast. One had to speak loud to make oneself heard above the seethe and bellow of the waves. During the March storms, spray had been known to leap skyward, sending a plume of cold white mist over the huddled gunners. But on summer nights, at the recession of the tide, there were moments of near silence, with the sea running far below, the foam driven on it like white leaves.

Falk held Danielle close: "I love you, I love you." The words seemed arrogant and trivial in the indifference of the night. But he went on heedless: "I am not bringing you very much. This carcass of mine and half a wedding present. The other half is lying in the gutter in the Rue de la Poissonnière. Let's leave it there. Half may be enough. I don't want to ask for the whole of life any more. Only for you, and for time enough to quarrel and make children and grow old together. If I have to, I'll even take

46

those four wicked daughters into the bargain. It's a bad bargain, Danielle, I know that. The merchandise has been damaged in transit. God knows you could do better. There must be fine young men about, with fine legs. Of your own people. Not the enemy, not the *sale boche*. There may be some around who could love you more blindly than I do. They wouldn't notice that your nose has grown a little too long. They might even make you happier than I can. But I won't let them have you. I want you. Utterly for myself. You cannot conceive how selfish I have grown. I believe with all my soul that I will make you happy. But I don't know whether that counts most. All I do know, all I care for, is that you are life to me, all of it I can grasp or make sense of now. I was a dead man when I first saw you, when you walked into my room that night. I breathed you in like air and began living. The presence of you inside me has kept me alive since. I love you, Danielle, selfishly and desperately. I cannot take no for an answer."

The vehemence of it held her rigid. But though she was afraid and uncertain, a bright malice flashed through her. "Say it in German," she demanded, "say it in German."

"*Ich liebe dich*, Danielle."

She shaped the words awkwardly for herself: "*Ich liebe dich*." They stuck in her teeth like a bitter rind. "It's not very beautiful that way. *Je vous aime* is better." She felt the tightness and impatience in his grip. "You are hurting me. Let go."

He did, and she swayed against the sudden gulf of night. "*Ich liebe dich*." She tried again and could not suppress an abrupt, unreasoned gaiety. "I would be Madame Falk. How strange. *Bonsoir, Madame Falk*."

"Danielle, come back to me. Come into my room, as you always did, with the morning sun. Put your hand on my sleeve. Tell me that you know what I'm asking for. That you love me."

She turned and took his head between her hands, staring at him for an instant as if he was a stranger; then she drew him

47

down swiftly. They stood gathered to each other. Even now, unsteady with delight and a great tiredness, Falk urged once more: "Tell me." He heard the words from a sudden closeness: "*Je vous aime.*"

At the foot of the cliffs the sea was beginning to simmer. They drew in the roused air and the salt lay sharp on their tongues. Holding Danielle fast, Falk told her of the blue pitcher. At first she did not remember. And when he told her of how he had buried it in the barn and of what it signified to him during the last months of war, rebellion stung her. He had planned it all. She had no existence of her own. She was part of a stubborn dream. She swerved back like a small angry flame: "I can't understand why you make so much of it. It was a cheap little jug. We never used the good china for our guests." She gave the word a fine edge of scorn.

But he seemed beyond her reach and she followed mutinous yet entranced as they clambered back up the cliff and struck out for La Hurlette.

"We must go to the barn, Danielle, and dig it up. I know we shall find it unbroken. I did not dare look before. Now I know. My love. My love." And he clasped her tight as they hurried through the trees.

Joined to his lunging step, Danielle felt herself in Falk's power. It gave her insidious content, as if she had been a swimmer who stops thrashing and yields to the seaward drag of the tide. But she could not let go entirely. The precariousness of their condition was too vivid in her mind. Too much of what lay before them was unanswered.

"Falk."

"Yes?"

"Even if it's true what we said back there, even if we are in love. . . ."

"Yes, Danielle?"

"What can come of it, Falk? They won't let us marry."

"Why not?"

48

"Because you're not one of us, and they look on me as a child. And it would do Nicole dreadful hurt."

"None of that concerns us, Danielle. Not really. I know it's true, but it can't be helped, and does it matter?"

"I don't think I would like to come with you to Germany. No. I don't think I would want to leave here. You mustn't ask it of me."

"Perhaps I will have to. And much more. Love is asking. All the time. For more than anyone ever dreamt of giving."

"I don't have that much to give, Falk."

"What there is I will take! Be warned."

She caught the lightness in his tone but also the obstinate desire. In the dark of the hedgerows his step seemed surer than hers.

"I'm afraid, Falk. I'm afraid."

"Of what?"

"I don't know. Of what they'll say in the village. Of your German friends. Of Jean. I fear his ghost. It will seek us out. It will harrow our lives. Don't laugh at me. It's God's truth. He will find us and damn us to hell."

"I am not laughing, Danielle. Perhaps he will come. In some way I wish he would. It would make my happiness more bearable. If we receive him into our lives, he will forgive us. Ghosts are watchdogs and children must learn to live with them in the house. And learn their language. I have heard it. They speak like snow."

"Father won't give us anything. If we leave here, I shall have to go as a beggar." "I know," said Falk gaily, "Monsieur Terrenoire made that quite plain. And here I came all the way from Hanover just to snatch your dowry. Think of it!" His laughter rang out.

"Be serious, Falk. There is so much against us. We are mad to carry on this way."

"I love you, Danielle." His voice left her naked. "Don't you understand? I love you. Everything you say is true. We are surrounded by absurd and hateful things. It will be even more difficult than you or I can imagine. Perhaps they will want to hang me and shave your head." She felt his fingers pass through her hair in rough solace. "I don't know whether I must go back to Hanover or whether we can live in France. But does it matter? I love you. And if I said it over and over all night long you wouldn't have heard the beginning of it!"

They moved in silence. Then Falk resumed. "You have a beautiful name. I will often call you in our house, not because I shall need anything, but to say it. Danielle. It's like a cool bright stone that has lain in a mountain stream."

"Please, stop it, Falk. I can't bear it. I'm too afraid."

They were nearly at La Hurlette. Falk entered the barn and advanced through the warm blackness with the surety of a blind man. Danielle saw him kneel in one of the old stalls now empty of horses. He scattered the crackling hay and the trodden dirt. Then he pried loose one of the floorboards and she heard the nails scrape. Suddenly he paused and she caught the tense pleasure in his voice. "Danielle, come here!" Once again she felt as if she had become a shadow to his being. She stepped nearer. "I have it. It's here. Exactly as I buried it." The object tinkled faintly as if the lid was loose. Falk brushed the dirt away cradling the little pitcher against his body. Then he rose triumphant. "It's unbroken, Danielle. It's been waiting for us all these years. My love, it's unbroken. Feel the edge. Not a chip. Take it. We shall drink from it in the mornings. Just as we used to."

He was reaching towards her when the beam of light struck between them. The pitcher shone blue and abrupt shadows sprang up the wall. Blaise was standing in the doorway, the lamp held stiffly before him. Danielle grasped the pitcher and bent away. The cows shifted in the hot still air.

Blaise strode in, breathing heavily. He rapped the girl across the mouth with the back of his hand, not in fury but bewildered scorn: "*Petite putain*."

Falk strained towards her but Blaise barred his way. He stood like a circus trainer, his powerful legs straddled: "I'm fed up. J'en ai marre. You're getting out of here. Tonight. You've made enough trouble. You're going to leave us in peace. We don't want you around here. Never again. I'm warning you. Get out while you can."

Falk flung out into the dark: "Danielle, tell him we love each other. Tell him we're leaving together."

"If she makes a move," said Blaise, "I'll beat the daylights out of her. But she won't move. She's just a stupid little goose. You may have turned her head with your fancy speeches. But she's coming to her senses. Look at her." He swept the light across her inert face.

"Danielle, tell him the truth. Come with me." She was staring at Falk but not seeing him. "For God's sake, Danielle, rouse yourself! Remember all that we've said, all that's happened. If I go now without you, I can never return." But she lifted her hands to her face and shrank from the light.

"Enough of this farce," said Blaise. "Get out of here. You can wait in the village. There's a bus to Rouen at daybreak. Get going, mon capitaine."

"Let me through to her," demanded Falk. "She's frightened of you. You're an ugly brute. But she loves me. Do you hear? She loves me! And nothing you can do will change that."

Blaise grinned. He knew his ground. When he turned to Danielle it was as if he had flicked a restive calf across the nose. "Why don't you say something to the handsome gentleman? He's waiting." He kept the lamp on her.

"Please," she moaned, "leave me alone. It's no good. They'll kill you if you stay. I told you it wouldn't do any good. You must go."

"Come with me," cried Falk.

"I can't. I don't dare. Perhaps I don't love you enough. Please let me be. Please." She kept her hands before her eyes, against Falk's anguish and the unswerving light.

Falk raised his cane but Blaise tore it from his grasp easily: "I could hammer your brains out right now. No one would care. But why bother? You're going to leave just like you came. Like a lame dog." He snapped the cane across his leg and threw the pieces into a mound of hay.

As he hobbled out of the barn, his hands clutching for support, Falk caught a last glimpse of Danielle. She had turned to the wall.

When she set out in pursuit of Falk late the next morning, Danielle was like a creature possessed. Only moments after he had been driven from the barn, a sense of utter desolation assailed her. She had run through the courtyard calling Falk's name under her breath. But darkness had swallowed him. She knew with the blinding certainty of pain that she could not endure without him. Her love was not the unbewildered glory he had demanded, but though imperfect, it made up the sum of life. Having come moments too late, this knowledge mocked her. The remembrance of her evasion and of Falk's crippled departure under the derisive flourish of Blaise's lamp, made her skin tight and cold. It was like a palpable nightmare and she could not shake it off.

Loathing herself, she stood under the chill heavy rain which began towards midnight as if it could scour her clean. Danielle watched from the arcade of the market hall as the dawn bus left for Rouen, but there was no sign of Falk. She hastened along the top of the cliff and stared vaguely at the woken sea. Then back to La Hurlette. She put on dry clothes and started out again, brushing Nicole aside as if she were an intruder.

As she hurried back to the village, the whole landscape turned into bleak unreality. The thought of not seeing Falk again filled her with wild misery. Yet she was afraid of meeting him. He would not forgive her cowardice and giddiness of mind. He knew her now for a shallow girl. He had said he would never come back.

Danielle began whimpering like a child. When she had been very little, she had been banished to her room for snatching rowdily at a sweet bun. After a time her father had come to the door. She could have her brioche if only she would express remorse for her wicked manners. Fighting back tears, Danielle had refused. On his way downstairs, Terrenoire casually popped the bun into his own mouth. Seeing it vanish, Danielle had felt the world collapse. She had howled with rage and sorrow. Now the same feeling of absurd deprivation engulfed her. She had thrown away her life in frivolous unknowing.

Ferreting about in Yvebecques, she found news. Between gulps of coffee Pervienne told her that when crossing his field, just after daybreak, he had seen a man hobbling down the road. He was leaning on what looked like a large dead branch. After a while the man had flagged down a truck and Pervienne had watched him clamber on to the back amid crates of lettuce and cabbage. Pervienne had an orderly mind. Wiping the last drop of coffee from the rim of the cup, he recalled that the truck bore the blue-and-yellow markings of the *Union agricole*. Doubtless it was on its way to Le Havre.

Only later, when the bus was actually entering the suburbs, did Danielle realize the futility of her search. The raids had torn great gashes in the city. Blocks of new, raw houses stood between stretches of vacant terrain. On the mounds of rubble the grass had a metallic sheen. The dust and clamour of construction lay thick in the air. As she hurried over upchurned roads, seeking out the garage of the *Union*, Danielle saw high cranes swing stiffly across the sky.

The garage was a cavernous hangar. Naked light bulbs threw a cold glare. In the far recesses the trucks stood hunched and silent. The dispatcher and the drivers were lounging in a small shed. Danielle rapped several times on the murky panes before they took notice. When they opened the door she smelled kerosene and wet leather. She asked whether any of them had seen a lame man; one of their trucks had given him a lift from

Yvebecques. He had been hobbling on a dead branch. Did anyone remember him, and where had they dropped him off in Le Havre?

The drivers looked at her and she drew her raincoat tighter. They told her to come in and get dry. The dispatcher rolled a cigarette and held it out. But she hung at the door asking obstinately. The man was very lame. He had red hair. Did no one remember? The drivers shrugged and glanced at each other. Finally one of them spoke up from the back of the shed. It was against company rules. But *merde*, the man could hardly walk and was worn out. So he had let him ride on the crates and when the rain had thickened had given him a sheet of burlap to burrow under. The dispatcher remarked sourly that the *Union agricole* was no bus line. Danielle asked: where had the man been set down? "I told him I could not be seen with a passenger near the garage," answered the driver, "so I dropped him off Boulevard Galliéni. There's a bakery on the corner. I saw him enter there."

A young trucker with blotches on his chin called out to Danielle: "Little lady, is he your lover?" "Yes," she said and hurried out of the garage.

One of the girls at the bakery remembered Falk. He had eaten several rolls standing at the counter. He had seemed ravenous and his clothes were sodden. He had left a puddle on the floor. The owner looked up from the apricot tarts and gave Danielle a sullen stare. Did anyone notice where he was heading? The girls giggled. Why should they?

During the ensuing hours Danielle wandered the city, now with directed intent, now in random circles, up and down the dust-blown boulevards, through the scarred streets, past the wharfs and corrugated-iron sheds, between warehouses and gantries, pausing in brief stupor on the freshly painted benches in the new playgrounds, and then hurrying on through the blind drifts of the afternoon crowd to the bus terminal and the railway station. She peered into *brasseries*, empty cafés and restaurants, treading the mill of the long day in a torment of loss and weariness.

A hundred times in the drag of hours Danielle saw Falk just ahead of her and ran towards him only to find a stranger in her path. His face and harried step seemed to leap at her out of the crowd; she saw it mirrored in the glass alembics in apothecary windows. Soon the city flickered in her sore eyes like the reels of a blurred film. Streets, building sites and quays revolved around her in a lazy, jeering motion, always the same, yet malignantly altered so that she could not be sure that she had already searched them out.

Looking up at the cranes, Danielle prayed for the miracle of momentary flight, imagining herself gyrating over the sea of roofs and streets, able to discern Falk and plummet upon him. Instead she plodded interminably and evening crowded at her with its delusive shadows.

She had tried to swallow a sandwich earlier in the day but it had gone stale in her mouth. Now a soft, sour nausea stirred in her throat. She sat on a fallen oil barrel and stared at the greying harbour. The rust flaked between her fingers, but she kept a stubborn grip and fought off dizziness. Suddenly she lowered her head and vomited. A great lightness overcame her and she felt a pang of hope.

Once again Danielle crossed the Boulevard Galliéni and circled the Place de la Libération. Hunger made her alert and quick. It rang in her head like a small chime. She began counting lamp-posts: "At the sixteenth I shall find Falk." And when the sixteenth had passed, she started over again with the same spurt of hope.

But after a time she stopped counting and began weeping helplessly. Despair stole on her as out of ambush. She had consumed the last of herself. The wine was spilt and she tasted the dregs and lees of her own being.

When she saw Falk she could no longer muster even joy. He was standing on a small wharf looking at the oil-flecked water.

He was leaning on an umbrella. Despite its massive old-fashioned handle, it had already bent under his weight. Danielle called to him in a dead voice. It did not carry and she sickened at the thought that he would turn away. She called again and stretched her hands towards him. He looked about and grew white as if he had seen that which was crying out in the midst and secret of his being gather shape in the evening air.

As they left the wharf, neither spoke. Only their fingers touched. They drank coffee in silence and looked in bewilderment at their own image in the misted silver urn. They said nothing to each other as they followed the *portier* up the stairs of the hotel. Falk's umbrella tapped on the worn tiles.

The shutters were closed but from the streetlights jagged shapes fell across the brown wallpaper and enamel basin. They sat in the musty quiet hearing the noise of day ebb from the city. At last Falk wrenched open the wooden blinds.

Searchlights were sweeping across the harbour like blue dancers. As Falk stepped back into the room Danielle rose. She guided his hands. Together they undid the buttons on her dress. The siren of a liner was singing westward. At first brazen and clear, then softly as if the sound had run into the sands of night.

The day of the wedding was unusually warm. The stone beach merged into banks of white haze. The first brown spots were appearing in the hedgerows, leaves burnt by the departing summer. The Terrenoires had assembled in the garden. Each had yielded in his own fashion. The old man had voiced muted approval: *Ce n'est pas une mauvaise affaire.* Madame Terrenoire had scarcely said anything. Events had come to pass as she foretold. She saw in the tumult and brusque conclusion of Falk's courtship proof of her divining powers. She kept the silence of an oracle and spent more time than she used to with Nicole. There was between them the unspoken discourse of conspirators. Both were old women now, gazing ahead to the bland pleasures of a common winter. To Danielle and Falk,

Nicole had come handsomely, wishing them Godspeed and seeking to make her presence no attainder to their joy.

Only Blaise was absent. He had shrugged off Falk's attempt at conciliation and had thrust his hands in his pocket. The day before the wedding he took his bicycle from the shed and said tersely that he was off to the market at Coutances.

Tante Amélie had come over from Harfleur. She was whirring about like a drunken bee when smoke has routed it from its hive. She scattered loud delight and the hem of her mauve dress billowed along the ground. At every instant she would clasp either bride or bridegroom to the large cameo brooch on her bosom. Her warm cheeks were streaked with tears. The dreary war had not been in vain. All had come well in the end. Tante Amélie had stitched a pale yellow gown for Danielle and presented Falk with a plum-coloured waistcoat. Now she darted about dusting off everyone in a whirl of order. Suddenly she peered at her pendant watch and sang out: *"Allons, enfants!"*

The party advanced through the orchard. They moved stiffly under the apple boughs, the women ample and flowery, the two men like sable penguins.

A few villagers were waiting in the silent chamber of the *mairie*. No one had taken the dust-cover from the chandelier. Monsieur Raymond, the mayor, was a spare, sallow man; but even he was perspiring. Having donned his tricolour sash, he read out the marriage service in a low, precise intonation. Danielle strained forward as if the grey words were of passionate interest. Falk's eyes wandered to the wall. From behind a dusty glass the General looked stonily on the proceedings. For a brief second Falk panicked. He could remember no French. But then he heard his own voice. Danielle assented in a whisper. Her lips were ash-dry, but as she embraced Falk, Tante Amélie vented a loud sob and Danielle began smiling.

Monsieur Raymond took off his glasses, wiped the moisture from the bridge of his nose and addressed the young couple. It was, he felt, an unusual, indeed, a portentous occasion. He would be doing less than his sworn duty if he did not call the attention of the newly-weds, of their family and friends, to the significance of the event. The Terrenoires had lived in Yvebecques longer than records showed. Monsieur Beltran, the clerk—*ce véritable savant*—affirmed that there were Terrenoires baptized and buried in the village in the seventeenth century. Monsieur Falk belonged to another world. He had come (here the mayor paused) in a manner—how should one say?—not altogether natural or beneficent. But Yvebecques had proved stronger than tragic circumstances. Its style of life, its renowned natural beauties, had entered into Monsieur Falk's heart. He had come back "over the hidden but unerring road of love". The mayor allowed the sentence to unfurl in the hushed room and looked at the ceiling. Might there not be in this, he asked, a lesson for the weary and divided nations? Here, in the *mairie* of Yvebecques, *notre petit village*, two young people had achieved what the captains of the earth sought vainly. "Yet, would Monsieur Falk forgive me if I add one further thought to this joyous hour? Even now and in this blessed moment, one should not forget the past. Like so many other families in the community, the Terrenoires bear witness in their bone and blood to the sufferings of France. *La patrie* had not wished for war, but thrice it assailed her. May this marriage be a portent of a more felicitous future. But may it also keep us in solemn remembrance of what has been endured."

Amélie sobbed again and Monsieur Cavel, the aged clerk, blew his nose. The mayor congratulated the happy couple and everyone filed into the open air. But no breeze stirred. Passing the fountain, Falk shifted his new lacquered cane and dipped his fingers in the water. He touched Danielle's lips. She nibbled the cold drops and the flush of desire that spread through her limbs was so strong that she leaned heavily against Falk's arm. The wedding party entered the café.

When they started out again for La Hurlette, the awkward silences had melted. The small glasses of tart red wine and the apéritifs were busy in the blood. Joined by further guests, the procession straggled through the village and towards the cliff. The gentlemen loosened their collars and tilted their straw hats against the veiled, relentless sun. The ladies advanced slowly, prickly and pouting for air. They called to one another; in the heat their voices crackled like dry grass. Danielle and Falk moved a little to one side. She sucked the moisture from her lips and kept her eyes to the ground as if seeking coolness in her own scant shadow. Falk felt sweat pearling down his collar and back; it chilled him. Beating against the chalk cliff, the air simmered. The birds had fallen silent, but among the hedges and wilted stalks wasps sang with a hum of low flame.

"I've lived here sixty-four years," panted Monsieur Cavel, "and never been so hot."

"It is unusual," allowed the mayor, "most unusual."

"One might as well be in the Sahara," said Siccard, combing back his flaxen hair, "I've been there, and believe me, it was no hotter."

"Ah, the Sahara," said Monsieur Cavel.

Estève, who was now married and putting on weight, stopped and stared at the banks of haze drifting along the cliffs and over the soundless sea. "*Ça va barder*," he announced, "there's bound to be one devil of a storm before the day is out."

"I hope so," said Nicole, "I'm stifling."

But Fridolin, who was bringing up the rear in a white linen suit, muttered: "Storms on a wedding night. A bad omen."

"*They* won't hear it," said Estève, trying to look roguish.

But no one responded or came fully to life until Tante Amélie called out: "*Courage, mes enfants*, we're nearly there."

The orchard was not much cooler, as if the sun had seeped into the shadows. Madame Terrenoire paused to tug at her corset. The men wiped the sweat from their faces and Monsieur Raymond closed his collar button. Nicole bore in on the newly-weds: "You must take the lead now." The smile on her lips was taut as in a bad photograph. Falk led Danielle to the gate and the mayor began clapping. Others joined, but in the stifling air the sound fell flat.

Everyone hurried under the trees and Amélie came into the garden carrying jugs of cider frosted at the rim. Siccard bellowed with pleasure. He raised his glass to bride and bridegroom, emptying it at one draught; the iced cider stunned him and his eyes blinked stupidly. The ladies drank with quick delicate sips and vanished into the house. Falk and Danielle drifted towards the shade of the barn. "I love you, Danielle." She did not answer but passed her fingers across his face in strangeness and wonder. They heard the clatter of dishes and the voices now more strident. Slowly they walked back to the long tables.

The food lay in garish heaps: bowls of dark blue mussels, steaming in milk; brick-red lobsters; fried mackerel bedded on ferns; plates of shrimp beside saucers of melted butter; larks, charred and spiky, cracking under one's teeth with a savour of game; two sides of beef sweating blood; tureens of fluffy white potatoes with warm napkins over them; watery endives; three cavernous bowls of dark green salad, shimmering with oil and nuggets of black pepper. Between the laden galleons, small boats and barks brimmed with spices, shelled walnuts and dried fruit. Long loaves were aligned on the sideboards next to squares of fresh butter, cold from the larder. There were wine and cider glasses before each plate, but soon the guests filled them indiscriminately.

A hot, ruttish wind blew across the tables. Terrenoire had scarcely tied the chequered napkin around his chin before thrusting his knife into a gamy paté and spreading it thick on a slab of bread. Then he drew towards himself a mound of shrimp. What had survived of lust in him was gluttony. Everyone followed suit. Cavel stuffed a lark into his toothless mouth and spat out the fine bones amid a howl of laughter. Madame Estève, a flushed stout woman with yellow eyes, carried the mussels to her lips, sucking them loudly. Melted butter dribbled down the mayor's chin as he leaned across the table. Fridolin carved the beef with wide flourishes and licked the gravy off his fingers. Monsieur Beltran had followed the main party after setting his wax seal to the marriage certificate; now he shovelled food into his gullet like a squirrel. He was the first to undo his braces. Other gentlemen did likewise and Madame Estève squealed happily as Cavel unhooked her dress. Danielle and Falk ate little.

Legs rubbed drowsily under the table and the wine grew warm in the uncorked bottles. Nicole could hardly keep up with the empty glasses and her skin glistened. Fridolin wavered to his feet; the wine was toiling in his brain and he moved his hands before his face as if he had walked into a cobweb. He ambled to Danielle and bent low, staring down her dress. "*Mon poulet*, let me tell you a thing or two about marriage. I am an experienced man." She felt his loud, liquorish breath at her ear. The mayor got slowly to his feet, sought to brush the crumbs and drippings from his rumpled shirt front and proposed the health of Monsieur and Madame Falk.

The day was wilting, early shadows drifted through the vibrant air. Toast followed on toast. The surfeited guests roused themselves as Madame Terrenoire and Tante Amélie brought in platters of pancakes filled with raspberry jam. The black, sweet jam was full of seeds and Siccard spat them through his teeth, now at the mayor, now at Nicole. She set down small glasses on the crowded tables and the *calvados* went from hand to hand. Under the blazing rush of the liqueur nearly everyone stopped eating. Only Terrenoire persisted, using his fork to snatch cold leavings as Nicole began carrying the plates back to the kitchen. Above the chaos of voices and clinking glass, Monsieur Raymond called for a word from the groom.

Falk pushed the dishes away from in front of him and rose, bracing his arms stiffly on the table. He looked down at Danielle and was startled to see her so withdrawn. He expressed his delight at the festive occasion and thanked all the distinguished guests for their presence. He raised his glass to Madame Terrenoire, to Nicole and to Tante Amélie, who had laboured to provide this noble feast. Cavel fluttered his spoon against a decanter. But Falk could not sustain the mock ceremonious note. He turned to the mayor: "Perhaps it would not be out of place, *Monsieur le Maire*, if I responded more particularly to your own eloquent words." Monsieur Raymond, who was trying to scrape a clot of jam from his trousers, looked up bleareyed.

"When I came back to Yvebecques, I was conscious of being a most unwelcome intruder. That is the burden we Germans must carry all over the world just now. And for a long time to come our children will have to carry it, though they had no part in our calamities. I have not tried to shed the load. I do not want to. But henceforth Danielle will help me to carry it and that is a kind of miracle." His hand rested momentarily on her shoulder. "I do not know yet where we shall make our home. But your village, Monsieur Raymond, will always be as close to me as it is to my wife."

Ma femme: it was the first time he used the word. It made him light of heart as if in victory. "Here in this garden," he went on; "here . . ."

"Under the ash tree, under the ash tree!" The voice stabbed at Falk exact and derisive. Blaise was hovering near the pigsty. With him were Lurôt and a coil of young men and women from the neighbouring farms. The voice sang out again like a javelin: "Under the ash tree. That's where you want to make your home, isn't it, *Herr Kapitän*!"

Falk sat down heavily. But the guests neither understood nor cared. They thumped the tables and called raucously to the new arrivals. Estève staggered over to Blaise with a glass of *calvados*. He lurched into one of the farm girls and spilled it down her brown neck. The girl bleated like a goat as Estève wiped her off, his fingers inside her blouse. The guests lumbered to their feet and the music began. Blaise had brought the fiddlers and

Lurôt blew his bagpipe. The sound skirled naked and hot through the descending twilight.

At first the revellers stomped awkwardly. Some dropped out. Cavel shuffled into the lilac bushes and was sick. Estève drew his wife towards the hayloft, tittering. But soon the music seized the dancers by the nape of the neck and flung them into motion. They moved in a fume of cider and sweat, their hobnailed shoes threshing the ground. Dogs who had been burrowing in the rank garbage turned and scurried between the dancers' feet. Flies swarmed out of the hedges.

Blaise danced with harsh abandon, lifting his partner from the earth and whirling her in jolting arcs. The girl's body lashed back and forth yieldingly in his grip and his face was set in cruel spite. The farmhands danced close, grinding their haunches into the flaring skirts. Now and again they strode back to the ravaged tables to pour cider down their parched mouths. Lurôt blew without halt. Driven by the acrid notes, starlings skimmed back and forth across the roof.

Beltran danced alone with the stilted precision of an old man. He brought his knees up sharply and held his hands above his head. The other dancers clapped to the beat of his mincing step. Faster and faster. He closed his eyes dizzily but kept whirling. Suddenly he faltered like a wearying top and stumbled sideways into Blaise. Blaise thrust him back to the hub of the circle. Out of control, the drunken clerk spun from hand to hand. He sagged towards the ground but they heaved him about. His mouth was open and gasping.

"Stop them," said Danielle, "stop them."

Falk paid no heed. The scene filled him with loathing. Yet it was unreal, like a clamorous nightmare. He was afraid, but could not comprehend his own fear. A desire to escape from La Hurlette and even from Danielle beat strong inside him. But he sat riveted, leaning on his cane and letting the cold rise in his back.

Amid hoarse outcries the men put the cider on the floor and

threw over the tables, clearing a wide space. The steaming air shook with their tread. Amélie's face appeared at the kitchen window. It was strangely white and she called out in protest, but her words were lost in the tumult.

"Let's go inside the house," said Danielle.

"Soon," said Falk. He scarcely knew what he meant. He was waiting for something to happen, something loathsome but of intimate concern to him. It was a feeling he had had once before, in those marshes near Smolensk. And he could not keep his eyes from the ash tree; its leaves seemed to grow thicker in the waning light.

The bounding couples had torn loose and all the dancers clasped hands in a single round. Glazed with drink and exertion, they swept on in wild orbit. Then the whiplash uncoiled. Before Falk could move, one of the young men had leaped over to Danielle, seized her by the wrist and whirled her into the circle. In the careening wheel her gown flashed like a scorched leaf. The blood ran heavy under Blaise's eyes and Nicole spun with her mouth agape.

The wind reared up without warning. It raked the farmyard with chill gusts. The haze scattered and the sky came down like lead. Large cold drops of rain splashed against the barn. The dancers wavered and one of the fiddlers began wiping his bow. Monsieur Raymond slipped away hurriedly. Falk rose with a surge of relief.

But Blaise yelled out: "One more dance! A bridal dance for the captain and his lady!" He came to Falk breathing hard: "Join our round. No man should let another dance with his bride. Not on his wedding night."

Falk stared into his red eyes. "I can't. You know that."

"Just once. A man can do anything if he tries hard enough. You've killed my brother and now you're taking my sister to bed. What's a little dance to a man like you? For old times' sake!"

Falk called to Danielle: "Let's go. You're getting drenched."

But Nicole barred his way: "Hold my hands. Come dance

with me. You can't deny me that. It's so little to ask." She hammered at him like an enraged child. "I shall never beg anything of you again, I promise."

"Don't be crazy, Nicole, it's impossible for me to dance." But hands tugged at him on every side and a voice shouted: "*Bravo la Wehrmacht!*"

Nicole dragged him into the circle. Falk looked for Danielle, but those who surrounded him were strangers and had faces like vacant masks. Lurôt had drawn close; he seemed to be blowing a single screeching note. It cut to the bone like the cry of a broken bird.

Falk strove to keep his balance but Nicole pulled him after her and the dancers began treading their mad round. He attempted to lunge out of the circle but it hemmed him in. As it whirled past, Falk saw Danielle fling herself at the barrier of arms and thrashing legs. He laboured towards her and struck wildly with his cane, but the wall of bodies threw him back. He stumbled and Nicole's hand slid from his grasp. He called desperately: "Help me, Nicole, help me!" But no one listened and Blaise's face spun around him, contorted with avid fury.

Falk started falling and heard Danielle scream. Her voice was coming closer and closer. He rose to meet it but the shoes kept smashing into his face. A wave gathered before him, higher and swifter than any he had ever imagined. It blacked out the whirling ash tree and Danielle's cry. Falk knew that the towering crest was about to break and engulf him. But beyond the green howl of water he glimpsed a trough of light. It was dim at first. Then it rushed upon him with a brightness he could not endure.

The dancers melted away under the downpour, bearing Danielle to the house.

After a time, Terrenoire shambled out to look at the dead man. He bent low gazing at his torn features. Blood was clotting in the fine red hair. He knelt as if to guard his guest from the rain, and spoke to him softly: "You came back too soon, Monsieur Falk, too soon."

Cake

1

War came to them hard. First, the Sunday cake grew smaller. Then the icing took on a grey, worn air, and crumbled under their teeth with a taste of ash. And now, on that first Sunday in March, rumour and unquietude sifted like fine dust through the parlour and corridors.

The guests of St. Aubain gathered for tea in tight knots. They threw wary glances toward the kitchen door. Instead of the cake, on the habitual large tray with its riot of lacquered cockatoos, there appeared Dr. de Veeld.

He was a small man with a high forehead and swift hands. He had the stoic verve of those who build proud, intricate sandcastles against a persistent tide. His reddened eyes took in the constrained group of men and women and he saw the edge of their expectation. He knew that their silence was rancour masked and ready to fly at him. Abruptly he smiled, in homage to the sharp-sighted malice of the adversary and in defence of his own failing.

"As you have observed, ladies and gentlemen, there is no cake."

He explained that the staff at St. Aubain, decimated as it was by flight and the demands of the military, had done their utmost to sustain the tone of the house, to provide, in the face of difficulties and chicaneries which he would not even care to describe, those comforts and graces of life which signified much to all present. But now was a time when the impossible could no longer be achieved. It would, he knew, come as a jolt to his guests (these being the kind of unpleasant facts he did not, as a rule, bring to their notice) that hunger was almost general outside the walls of the park.

At this the Owl interrupted in her hoarse, insistent voice: "I know. It's no news to me. I know because the dogs don't bark any more at night."

Dr. de Veeld continued as if he had not heard. Up to now, it had been possible to scrape up enough margarine and sugar to manage cake on Sunday afternoon. It could no longer be done. What rations the *Kommandatur* in Liège allowed would barely suffice to cover the essential needs of staff and patients. As always, he bracketed the word with a momentary pause. Were it not for the arbour and vegetable garden, to which several of the ladies and gentlemen now gathered had shown admirable devotion, the situation would be even more drastic. With care and some sacrifice, St. Aubain would be able to weather the coming months. No one could see further ahead. But he did not believe that the terrible events outside could last beyond the summer. After which it might again be possible to have cake and, indeed, other delicacies, on Sunday afternoons.

De Veeld walked back to his office and the kitchen-maid, an old woman with sallow skin, brought out the pale tea and the cups. She was deft at parcelling into each a wisp of coarse grey sugar. The milk was thin as smoke.

The patients lingered, many not drinking. They stared at the sideboard where the cake should have been and the sense of deprivation mounted in them, making their spirits acrid. One man stood by the window gripping the heavy blackout curtains, now drawn. The March light lay cold on the gravel walk. He began weeping loud and the tears stained his shivering wrist.

The Owl, a tall, spindly woman, whom the staff knew as Madame Alice, moved sharply among her friends: "It's intolerable. We pay a great deal here. I know I do. There is always butter to be had somewhere. The farmers hide it, in the loft. But he's telling the truth about everyone being hungry out there. Remember what I said about the dogs. None of you would listen. But I don't sleep nights, so I know what's going on."

70

The Grays, who inhabit the twilit zone of partial infirmity, and who at St. Aubain, as in similar institutions, were of vital aid to the inadequate staff, finally drank their tea. But the boy with the thin hair tore the single crocus out of the vase on the mantlepiece and stamped on it. Then he began calling in an un-wavering tone: "Where is our cake? It's Sunday. It's Sunday."

2

I knew nothing of all this when I was first brought to sanctuary, before daylight, a week after Dr. de Veeld's announcement. I knew only the stench and smother of my fear. They held me closer than the strait-jacket or the injection which, though a mild dose, made my features so vacant that the German patrols, who twice stopped our gloomy progress to flash their lights under the canvas flaps of the small truck, flinched away in distaste.

I am an American. I found myself in Angers at the outbreak of war, writing a dissertation on the style and syntax of Garnier, the neo-classic tragedian of the sixteenth century. I say this without either embarrassment or that feline humility affected by minor scholars who burn, in their inmost, with a desire to be critics or poets. I have an exact mind and tenacity, but my reach is small. Yet if literature is the only true mirror held up to the condition and gist of our souls, then those who polish some minute blur on its radiant surface or mend a crack at its sharp edge, are not without merit. Some heat falls even in the shadow of a bright day.

I stayed on in France not only because there were decisive manuscripts unexamined (particularly with regard to Garnier's knowledge of Italian Senecan drama), but because the home-ward tug was faint. Neither the house I had inherited in Rock-port, nor the vague expectation that I would enter my uncle's insurance firm, seemed real beside the task in hand and the muted charm of Angers and the Loire. I have private means.

At first the war seemed remote, and even when the occupation came, in June 1940, my life scarcely altered. The authorities behaved with propriety and allowed me to travel to Paris quite often to work in the rare book room at the Bibliothèque Sainte-Geneviève. I have always loved that room for the leap of afternoon light through its high, veiled windows.

But one evening, the unheated, blacked-out train in which I was returning to Angers, halted suddenly in a small wood. An SS patrol combed it from end to end, irrupting into each compartment. Across from me sat an old man and a girl. As the searchers stomped nearer, sweat trickled down his lips and hands. The officer handed back my American passport with a slight flick of the head. He scrutinized the old man's papers for several minutes, and the old man's body gave off a sharp smell. Then the guards thrust him out of his seat, not in rage, but with venomous pleasure. They pushed him down the steps of the railway car and he stumbled to his knees by the side of the track. They struck him with unhurried blows, let him lurch to his feet and kicked him to the ground again.

The girl raced out of the compartment and lunged at them. They held her down and rubbed cinders in her face till it was black and raw. Then the train began moving. I do not recall what happened in the next few instants, but I found myself in the latrine vomiting.

Yet the image gripped me. It dimmed my mirror when I shaved in the brown-upholstered room at the Pension du Roy Henri, and it lay, like a flickering stain, on the pages of the Garnier manuscript. I saw them rubbing the cinders into her hair and mouth, and though I had lost them from sight as the train began rolling, I felt certain I had seen them pull off her coat. I knew that something bestial and slow had come to pass in that leafless wood. The remembrance sickened me, but it also brought a queer warmth and drew my skin tight.

Each time I travelled to Paris after that, I waited for the train to reach the stand of ash and scrub-oak where we had stopped. As it entered the wood, my excitement mounted. The blood raced in my ears and I had to leave my seat and stride up and down the corridor. Pressing my fist against my closed lids, I could see the night group with utter sharpness, the old man being thrashed and the officer picking up cinders and gravel in his gloved hand.

When I returned to my seat and sought to resume work on the texts or glossaries I carried in my Harvard bag, the letters danced before my eyes. I must have looked strange for everyone stared at me. But I anticipated each journey with obscure thirst. I could have finished the chapter on Garnier and the theme of vengeance, but kept it incomplete. The American Consulate wrote me that it was advising all nationals to return home; the letter gathered dust in my bureau drawer. It seemed as irrelevant as my memories of the three elms and the yellow awning in the backyard of my mother's house in Belmont. But the cinders burned my skin and I woke nights shivering with an unclean sweetness.

I was afraid. But more than that, I was envious: of the old man and the girl by the side of the track, of the torments being wrought on them. Of what I supposed had been done to them once they had been dragged to the SS barracks, and then afterwards. Not supposed—knew. For by the late summer of 1941, and in the fall, the correctness of our hosts had worn thin. Even in the stillness of Angers there could be no doubt. Those who had been taken from their houses at night turned up in the rushes of the Loire, their faces and bodies torn. One had to be deaf not to hear the wolves in the wind.

But my envy grew like a cancer. It made my very soul itch. Looking back on that time (and nothing in my life has been more vivid), I can hardly give a sane account of my feelings. I was living an unsavoury dream. I wanted to be that man. I cried out in my prim solitude for those heavy blows. Imagining the rake of cinders on my face, I grew dizzy and had to grasp the edge of my enamel wash-basin. With a scholar's ferreting nose, I scanned all I could glean from the censored newspapers of hostages, deportations and the rising ferocity of German reprisals. The military were beginning to put up placards with the names and pictures of those executed. I stood before them in mournful lust. I memorized their features and relived, in the privacy of my room, what I could conceive of the obscene torment of their several deaths. I envied them crazily. Yet at the same time, I sweated fear.

For I have always been a physical coward. My childhood was marred by cowardice, by my inability to climb walls, by the panic that held me rigid at the edge of a diving-board. I tried fiercely to be as bold and easy as other boys. I forced myself up rock spurs in the New Hampshire hills and rode my mother's large, unsteady mare. But she caught the scent of my fear and threw me. So I grew sly and scuttled like a lizard to my books and the refuge of our garden when my cousins went out to steal apples or dared each other to skate the loosening ice on Mattackwa pond.

Physical pain was a nightmare and I was afraid of the holidays because I knew my mother would take me to the dentist. By some insidious betrayal, my mind seemed capable of storing up past hurts; they ached and stung in remembrance. In school, they jeered at me and called me Killer.

Reading reports of the *maquis* and of what happened to those who fell into Gestapo hands, I twitched with fear. Somewhere I had heard, or perhaps imagined, that they made prisoners insert their fingers in the jamb of a door and then slammed the door shut. The wild tear of pain, the bone splintering, infected my dreams. I often awoke moaning and wet.

But envy was shriller than my fears. I wanted to be one of those men. It seemed to me a deprivation, the omission of a rare chance, that I should not have visited on my own flesh and nerve the hideous contrivances they had experienced. We live at the airy top of the spiral staircase of our inward; only the great fears and pains can force us to the long descent. Yet who has not been in the well of his being, in the foul lightless place, has taken no journey. Not to know how you will behave when you are strung on the bench and they walk towards you with their gloves, is to know little. It is to live with yourself as spinsters do, in the brittle familiarity of mere acquaintance.

The dramas of Garnier are blood red. Now there was a bridge between the antique matter of my labours and what was actually happening around me, in the prison camps and in the cellars of the Rue de Lorraine. How could I apprehend the cry of the blinded and the torn, as it rose from the still page, unless I had heard it in my own throat?

But these were hypocrisies. I was riveted to a puerile, mad fancy. I could not keep my mind from the thought of how marvellous it must be to have endured. Already there were legends of couriers and *maquisards* who had kept silent under torture, who had spat in the face of their tormentors and then locked their teeth. Some had survived or even been released, too broken to be of use. To be one of these, to have walked the entire length of the tunnel and to have come out into the light, seemed to me consummation prouder than any dreamt of by lover or poet. After that there would be no more fear; the furies would no longer threaten but walk by one's side like old watchdogs.

I detest club dinners and college reunions. But during that late summer in Angers, I spun a fantasy so intense and detailed that it became the centre of my existence. I saw myself at a Harvard commencement, joining the other members of my class behind Widener Library for the alumni procession. It would be one of those hot, still days when the light dapples the elm leaves and straw hats in Harvard Yard with flecks of green and gold. The class marshal would lead us past the great flight of steps. Some around me had wilted and grown stout; others preserved their greyhound air. But all kept a gentle, wary pace so as not to hurry my progress. They knew how heavily I leaned on my cane and what austere panache I showed in being with them at all.

As we paraded under the blue shadow of the spire, women turned their heads slightly and stole a glance at me and whispered. For I had borne the worst that can be flayed and charred on a man's body, borne it eleven days unyielding. On the last day, the SS major had lifted his hand towards the rim of his cap in covert salute. I had been on the other side of the gate; my sinews were rent beyond repair, but all dread had been cleansed from me. Hearing the quick hush of voices wherever I went, in my mother's drawing-room on Thursday afternoons, when the committee of the Fairfield Club met, among the clerks in my uncle's office, or in the rare book room at Houghton, where I was putting final touches to my definitive edition of Garnier, I kept a shy mien—but my soul sang loud in its depths.

I rehearsed this vision, I revelled in its every detail. It furnished my dank room at the pension and warmed me when I walked along the deserted banks of the Loire. It became the thing worth living for. At any cost. So I spent my days between fear and desire, between hysterical imaginings of pain, and a secret longing. If it is granted us to live on earth some stretch of our damnation, I must, in those months, have won remission of Hell.

The trap closed softly. As if I had taken a Sunday stroll into the Gobi desert.

There was hardly any paraffin left for the small stove in the reading-room. To keep warm I took quick turns around the *Cour de la Mairie* with its ornate sundial and bust of Ronsard. One afternoon an elderly woman followed me. I recognized her for she had come several times to sit in the chair next to mine at the library. She had a green cardigan and chafed, wavering hands. She asked me whether it was true that I was an American, and without pausing for an answer: "Will you help?"

Others had asked, but they sought something banal: a note

commending them to the consulate in Marseille, or the chance to barter an old book or engraving (I was known to covet such things), for the cigarettes and cooking-fat I occasionally received in half-ransacked parcels. Here was something else, finer-edged.

Would I take a volume of poems to Paris? They were oddly underlined. A man would meet me at the number forty-eight bus station outside the Gare d'Orléans and ask me whether I liked the white wines of the Loire valley. I was to hand him the book and take another in exchange. This she would collect from me, under the library arcade, the following Tuesday.

Though the device seemed to me stale, as in an old film, I felt a jab of fear and excitement. She saw me hesitate and asked again. There was a harried pride in her manner. They did not like to entangle outsiders in their affairs. But help was badly needed. I would be running little risk. An American, carrying scholarly books, would pass the gauntlet of French militia and German guards unquestioned. We were neutrals. She flushed, as if the statement was itself an indecency.

That is how I became a courier for one of the numerous networks of amateurs and trained agents which were then being formed, in spurts of roused hatred and mutual distrust, throughout France. Our *réseau* consisted mainly of radical or marginal Catholics. Several of our most valuable informants were men of the lower clergy. They acted their part with the zest of schoolboys who have slipped over the seminary wall into the sun. Threading through the hedge country on their bicycles, they brought warning and solace. We were supposed to be in disciplined touch with a larger organization to the south, and ultimately with London. But I doubt whether the web was that strong-woven.

I was content. My dreams were proud and did not wake me.

My first three journeys were placid. But one late afternoon in November, at Châteaudun, a girl entered my compartment (I always travelled first class to make the unruffled ease of my American status more apparent). She was shivering and her

77

legs were scratched raw, as if she had been caught on wire or climbed a sharp paling. She asked me whether the first snow had fallen in Boston. That was the signal prescribed in our somewhat romantic code. Then she bent forward as if to brush the dirt off her shoes, and told me that we would have to jump off the train when it slowed down in the marshalling yard, before entering Paris. The Germans had wind of our coming.

She must have seen how afraid I was and said there was nothing to worry about. The train moved at a crawl when rounding the last curve and it was not much of a drop. She had done it often. She said it without mockery, but seeing my hands shake she looked away embarrassed.

I fell stiffly and tore a muscle. She helped me over the maze of tracks and in the rain and darkness we passed unobserved. We spent the night in an empty apartment in the *banlieu*. Sitting on the mattress, she told me that the easy times were over. The hunters were getting cleverer and more savage. A number of clandestine groups such as ours had been infiltrated and destroyed. She went to the lightless window, her back to me: "You've done more than we had a right to ask. Perhaps it's time for you to go home, to your own people. I am sure the first snow *has* fallen in Boston." I was grateful, but hated her cool voice.

And, of course, it was too late. They routed me out of bed before daylight on 8th December and took me into hiding. When the police called at the pension, they found only my soiled linen and a summer suit. I left my notes and the two completed chapters of the Garnier study with the landlady. She stashed them in the attic, beside a red rocking-horse. I shaved my small beard and was given a set of false papers. Staring at my naked lips in the mirror, I found their expression sly and feeble. I loathed my assumed identity. I had slipped into an alien skin and it rubbed my nerves. When I saw the girl again, at a farm on the outskirts of Angers, she said: "You are one of us now." But I wasn't, and because she knew it her tone was irritable. They grudged me what claims I had to their anguish.

This time, I travelled to Paris on a farmer's truck. We carried potatoes which were frozen and smelled of rain. The *réseau* found work for me in an antique shop. I was to prepare inventories and catalogues for appraisal or auction. But the hours were empty and I lived in dread of the night when there were tracts to be distributed or messages to carry.

Why did I not break my tenuous, amateurish link with the underground? Paris is an inland sea with deep, brackish pools. Keep your head down and you're safe. I might have slipped into southern France or even tried to buy my way across the Spanish border. What drove me to take chances for which I had neither sufficient nerve nor blindness?

The girl played a part. Her solicitude enraged me. But the cause of my feverish inertia lay deeper. I must have believed, in the secret place of vanity, that the game could be won unscathed, that it would not exact its price.

The warren of the city gave odds to the hunted. The Germans stabbed out after us, but we slid between their fingers like dry sand. Every time I went to distribute a clandestine tract or help move the parts of our transmitter from one loft to another, in that humped sea of grey roofs, I caressed the image of my heroics. I whispered to myself that this was the last hazard, that I could withdraw at will into the warming light of remembered danger. In the vacant shadows of the warehouse, where I dusted and catalogued the seven-branched candelabra of the deported and the dead, I fancied the high grace of my return. Though Paris was dark that winter, I saw, from the corner of my eye, the tawny gold of the elms on Brattle Street. And I heard the voices: "You stayed on in France after we entered the war, didn't you? Is it true that you were in the underground? That *is* a rosette in your buttonhole." And the women asking: "Is it true they did things to you, terrible things?" I practised a shy nod, and gestures of diffident avowal.

The nearness of my obsession fascinated me. We never spoke

79

of torture. Allusions to what had happened to friends or contacts taken in the net and brought to the Gestapo cellars, were harshly suppressed. In the Rue de la Pompe and the Avenue Jean Jaurès, parents sat by their children at night and put cotton in their ears. Men had been known to scream for twelve hours; their voices cracked through the pavement like thorns. But we said nothing to each other. Every man acted as if he held a talisman or bond of fate. The thing would not happen to him. Yet the thought hovered in one's mind constantly and seeped like marsh gas into our brave, clipped words. Often, in the midst of a briefing, or when we scattered on our night errands, the image of torture, the stifled conviction that it lay in near ambush, made the room prickly and cold, as if a lamp had dimmed. Then we saw each other naked.

Soon my excitement, my modish display of nerve, gave out. Nightmares won't let themselves be fondled; they lurch into reality like huge, stinking cats. Fear shrilled in me. I lay at night dreaming the lash and rose in the morning with the grit of panic in my mouth. I could think of nothing else. I lost weight and my urine darkened.

I was afraid. I was hideously afraid. To keep a hold, I sought to convince myself that the pain would be endurable, that the rumours which filtered through to us were exaggerated. If the things recounted were true, and not the mere brain fever of a period sick and damned, a man would pass out quickly. What was the use of that if you wanted information from him? I do not smoke, but scrounged for cigarettes so I could touch my hands and stomach with their glowing tips. I passed a nail file over my teeth till I shook with nausea. But my fear only grew worse; it lived in me like a stench.

On the 26th of February, the Gestapo seized our transmitter. Two men and the girl were in the attic when they smashed down the door. One man threw himself out the window, but they manacled the two others before they could move. They dragged the girl down four flights of steps head-first.

When I heard the news, my nerve broke. I realized that my fantasies of heroism were a fraud, that I was contagious with fear and betrayal. I knew with certainty that I would howl at the first blow. I would whine and creep before them and kiss their hands and boots. I would tell them everything they wanted to know, every name, every contact, every location. There would be no need to tie me to the bench. I would yell out everything, at once. They would stare down at me in derision, kick me in the belly as if I was a dead, bloated marmot, and let me go.

It is not easy for me to remember that week or set it down in words. Is it possible that the hysterical creature who scurried from one member of the *réseau* to the next, begging for safety, for release, for a drug with which to glide into painless death, was I? Did I try to hang myself on the night of the 27th (when we believed that the man had yielded under their torments and that our names were out) and merely fall from the chair losing control of my bowels? God's image may dwell in each of us, but it has precarious lodging.

The next morning they pounced on one of our couriers. Foolishly, the man had contacted his *concièrge* in order to recover from his apartment, now a mouse-trap, his winter coat. We were ordered into immediate hiding. Together with an old type-setter, who had done most of our illegal printing, I was sent to Lille. We spent five days burrowed in the back room of a grotesquely ornate garden house. At every footfall obscure shocks went through me and my stomach turned. I sweated in the cold.

We crossed the frontier with false papers and were harboured in a convent in Charleroi. A group of *maquisards* was active in the gorges and thick woods of the Ardennes. We were invited to join them. But I was burnt out. I thought that in some moment of unbearable fear I might run into the street and throw myself at the mercy of the first German patrol. I had grown loathsome to myself and dangerous to the hounded remnants of our group.

A man they called Sambre came to see me. He said that he too had been at a university, working on early Flemish art. In the far background of the paintings of Christ's agony there were always blue mountains, or meadows tranquil under the morning star. He felt these were important.

We walked in the cloister and looked at the wet snow. He was not angry, only tired. He said there were casualties of every kind; some could be infectious. He had been in touch with a rest home. It was a good hiding-place and they had used it before to guard British airmen on their run to the coast. Dr. de Veeld could be trusted; he had been one of the first to conspire against German rule. I could lie hidden until war's end or until the Gestapo called off the chase. All I need do is to feign idiocy for a few hours while they brought me to Liège. They would give me a drug. I tried to tell the man of my shame, but he left abruptly.

Two sisters of the Order of the Sacred Heart conveyed me. Lying in the truck, confined and numbed, I gazed on their starched coiffs. I dreamt vaguely of the Irish king borne westward by white gulls. Perhaps I have a pompous imagination.

That is how I came to St. Aubain.

3

"Don't you understand? He *has* butter. And there are packets of sugar in the bottom drawer of his dresser. Under a cambric handkerchief. Good God, I've seen them. Why doesn't he let us have any? He keeps it locked. He's sly as an eel. But I swear to you I've seen them."

She drilled the words at me.

"It made the week go by. I couldn't have stood it otherwise. On Saturday morning they stirred the batter. And they baked in the afternoon or sometimes in the evening, when they thought I was asleep. But I don't sleep. Heaven knows how much they licked from the bowl before putting it in the oven. It smelled like summer. Knowing it would be there, on that sideboard on Sunday afternoon, made the week go by."

She combed the rust-grey hair from her ears: "How dare he treat us this way? I want you to know I pay a great deal here. I could not bring the dresses. But you should see me in the bronze chiffon. And in the organdie. They are in the tallboy in my bedroom in Bruges. Oh I knew I should have brought them. I hoped I would be among refined people. I could no longer endure the things that came by in the canals. I watched at night. I saw what they were doing in the streets. So they came to demand my house. Did they take yours? But I mustn't think of those dresses and the Persian shawl. Dr. de Veeld has forbidden me to think of those things. I have heart-flutters. I tell you that because you are a refined person. What right has he to treat us so abominably! Don't you understand? There are squares of butter under his cambric handkerchief. We must help each other."

Madame Alice turned away. Then she flapped back at me with a hoarse moan: "I'm hungry. Don't you understand? I'm hungry."

Sudden safety unnerves. During my first days at St. Aubain, I moved in a furry half-sleep. On the railway to Boston, Route 120 is the last stop before South Station where the chauffeur would be waiting for me in the old, gleaming Dodge. I knew he would be there, brushing the snow off my mother's plaid blanket. And the Christmas holiday lay before me; an immensity of ten days in my own bed, with its stiff, fresh sheets, and the nutmeg grater, and the toboggan rides down Concord hill.

When the train pulled away from Route 120, I shut my eyes tight and pretended that we were going the *other* way, that my mother had seen me off, crumpling the wet handkerchief into her glove, and that I was heading back to Choalten. I hated the school with a hatred that still leaves me shaken. Thinking that the holiday was over, that I would, in a few hours, be back in purgatory, with its reek of sawdust and wet bath-towels, I drove myself to the verge of tears. In that instant, the conductor would sing out "South Station." I opened my eyes and could see Oscar, silvery and smiling, lifting his cap. Before I knew it, I would be wrapped in the Shetland blanket, speeding home. The game made me limp with delight.

I played it now, in the stripped arbour and behind the kitchens. I imagined that the Gestapo was at my heels, that I was trapped in my room at Angers. I could hear the grating breath of their dogs. But when I took my hands from my face, there was only a garden and a gravel walk, or Dr. de Veeld looking past me from the window of his office. And far off, the widow's voices of the bells at curfew.

A man with florid cheeks tugged at me: "The Owl has been croaking to you. You believe her, don't you?" He stared with heavy scorn. "The woman's sick. She never had a house in Bruges. It's all lies. She worked in a hotel kitchen. Yet she acts as if she had rights around here."

A thin trickle slid from his full, jeering lips. He could not retain it and his chin twitched: "But she's telling the truth about the cake. Sometimes they made mocca icing, with candied flowers. In every second flower they put a walnut. Those of us who have some decency had worked it out. Whoever had a slice with a walnut one Sunday would take one without the week after. But not the Owl! She cheated like a scullion. She popped the thing in her rotten mouth before anyone knew what had happened. It made me ill. I wanted her to choke on it. I wanted it to stick in that scrawny gullet of hers. But why have they taken it away from us?"

He put his wet lips to my ear: "Speak to de Veeld. You're new. He'll listen. Why is he hoarding the butter and the sugar and the walnuts?" He gripped my arm. "I can't forget the smell; it was all warm." He gave a flustered laugh, but would not let go till his knuckles grew white.

4

De Veeld knew, of course. He had made my rescue possible. But he treated me with so scrupulous a composure that I sometimes winced. I realized that the mask had to be worn while others were about. Yet I longed for some private signal of our complicity. Whenever we crossed, in the parlour or dining-room, I tried to draw from his polite mien an intimate wink, an admission of the bleak privilege of my status. I wanted this man to signify plainly, even if only between ourselves, that I was not mad.

After a week I lost patience. I waited outside his consulting-room and asked point-blank whether he did not wish to see me. He looked up, surprised, and said "No".

Like the milder cases, I was assigned odd jobs around the house and in the garden. Our rations had thinned and I too was hungry. The ghostly remembrance of a cake I had never eaten made my mouth water.

One afternoon I was weeding among the pale rhubarb and the radish beds by the wall. A thin fog lay in the branches. The work was light, but a sour queasiness heaved inside me. My skin was wet and my legs fluttered like an old man's.

The birds had been at the grape bushes. A girl was coaxing the scraggly vine back on to the trellis. She glanced over and took a sliver of bark from her pocket: "Put it in your mouth and chew on it. You'll feel better." It had a wry taste. "It's hard at the beginning. Until you're used to being hungry, I mean. But soon it'll stop gnawing. It just leaves one feeling a little cold, even in the sun."

I remember her as I shall remember nothing else in my life. She was slight of stature, and her features were fine-drawn, as if the brusque agony of late events had set on them a steady shadow. She had high, delicate cheek-bones. Her eyes were large and deep-set. They had in them a glint of wary malice, like the eyes of a fox when the light is grey. The shock of her tense grace passed through me. Only her hair was strange. In its natural darkness lay crude strands of bleach.

She saw my eyes on it and turned away amused: "My father emptied the whole bottle on my head before they came for me. When I arrived here it was like burnt flax. But it doesn't last." She pushed the heavy black curls from her temple and laughed in a remembrance so private as to shut me out entirely. Later that low, guarded laugh often came between us. Hearing it the first time, I felt a sharp longing and pressed my fingers against the wall. I must have looked as if I was about to be sick for she stepped nearer: "Is anything wrong? Do you want to sit down?"

"It's you."

"I?"

"You're very beautiful. I think you're the most beautiful person I've ever seen."

She brushed her hands down her skirt: "Not here. Please. There are enough mad people about."

Her flat tone jolted me. I realized suddenly that she too was an outsider, that we both stood above the tideline. The dead, green smell of the undertow hung close, but we were miraculously on shore.

"You're not . . ." The word was like grit.

"Insane? No. No more than you." And she turned back to the torn fruit. Her gestures were exact and contained. But every few moments there pierced in them a surge of pure, bounding life. She carried her small, swift body as against a hidden wind. Everything in me seemed to break open at the sight of her, at the low, clear chime of her voice. I was happy. In that pitiful garden, amid the hungry and the mad, I was happy as noon.

"Don't stare at me." She said it smiling.

"I can't help it. To find someone like you here. . . ."

She lowered her head: "Perhaps I was pretty. People said so. I don't know. But I don't want to be any longer. I don't even know whether it's right that I should be alive here, like a scared

86

rabbit in a hole. Not when all the others . . ." She stabbed at the vine and looked away: "Don't pay attention to me. I talk too much. I didn't mean that you're hiding because you're afraid. I am thinking of myself. You see, they've taken father and Jacob. And now there's no news from mother or from David. He's my younger brother. He's the baby."

Her eyes stared wide and unseeing: "Surely they wouldn't take David. He's only fourteen. My God, they wouldn't take him, would they?"

Hearing her was like holding a live coal in my hand. I looked down helpless. I said that I didn't know, that I had run away because I couldn't bear the thought of physical pain.

"But David's only a child. Why are they taking the children? Oh God, why are they taking the children?" Her body shook with angry desolation, and I stooped low over the frozen weeds.

"I'm sorry I wailed at you. I don't usually. But seeing someone from the outside. Someone who knows. That's the awful thing about being here. Most of them don't realize what's happening on the other side of the wall. No more cake on Sunday. That's all it means to them. What right have they to be at peace? They're taking the children now, aren't they? I can read it in your face. And here everyone walks around in a great stillness, not knowing. When I was a little girl and caught cold, they gave me a syrup. It was so warm and sweet you could taste the sleep coming with it. It must feel like that when the mind sleeps, all warm and dark. You see, I talk too much. And I get mixed up in my own words. But soon you'll know what I mean. Being here is like running around in a nightmare. You know there's something hideous just behind you. You shout at people and shake them; but they just walk by in their own dreams, smiling."

"How did you know about me?"

"Sometimes Dr. de Veeld tells me things. He's taking terrible risks. The Germans have been here once already; they came with their dogs. I was working in the kitchen and one of them patted my fine blonde hair: *echt Flemisch*."

"You admire Dr. de Veeld very much, don't you?"

She heard the scratch in my tone and looked puzzled: "Of course. Who wouldn't? He came for me only a few hours before father was taken away. I didn't want to go. I fought and bit in the car. I tried to jump out. Later I was horribly ashamed. But he's never mentioned it." She was again beautifully in control of herself: "Of course I admire him."

My new, absurd jealousy must have shown.

"Don't make a face like that. Now you really look ill."

"What does our eminent doctor say?"

"That you have a minor infection. Outside the walls it might be contagious. But not here."

I hacked the ground. After a few moments she said she had work to do in the main building. We would meet again in the refectory. Moving through the mist, she seemed a far-off personage in a silk landscape.

I called out in pure desire: "Wait. What's your name?"

She hesitated, as if I had touched her: "My name is Rahel."

5

We were together that evening, our shadows close in the failing light. The high, rich note of her being held me utterly. The tale was a horror, but in those days common.

The Jakobsens had lived in a large house in the suburbs of Brussels. It had a garden with laburnum and dark tulips. Inside were a Bechstein and a music-stand with Chopin études. There were two Chagall still-lives, early, sinuous water-colours on the walls, and books in many languages. There were servants downstairs and festive candles. Monsieur Jakobsen often took the wheel with the chauffeur beside him when driving to the Bourse in the morning. There were uncles from Frankfurt and sleigh-rides and long summers on the beach at Le Zoote.

Samuel Maagen, Madame Jakobsen's brother, came from Antwerp and would show Rahel and David small uncut diamonds in silk paper. Sometimes he had spoors of glittering dust on his thick waistcoat. Rahel had a childhood friend, Annie Landau. Their intimacy was full of fierce secrets. Holding hands, they prowled the verge of the golf course at Waterloo and whispered. At Christmas the families raided each other's houses and built a snow-man in the garden, placing on his mad moon-face, amid shrieks of annual delight, the large-brimmed hat Monsieur Landau had worn as a boy in Odessa. The Landaus and the Jakobsens still went to the synagogue once or twice a year, but in black English homburgs.

When Uncle Joseph and Aunt Ruth had to leave Frankfurt, they stopped at the house on their way to America. They had been allowed only one suitcase. Aunt Ruth came down to dinner in her high-laced walking-shoes. The new maid stared at them. Rahel flew at her in a rage and ran to her room. She lay on the wide, soft bed, with its pattern of strawberries, and wept uncontrollably. Her father sat by her, held her cramped fingers and told her not to be afraid. There had been bad times before. That summer there was barbed wire at the end of the beach, and Annie Landau's cousin—with whom Annie was grievously in love—emigrated to Brazil.

It all came as quickly as if a break in the power line had plunged the house, with its rich weave and legacy of life, into blackness. Soon Rahel was kept home from school. They sat in her mother's room, driven from the chill, dust-gathering spaciousness of their former ways. Monsieur Jakobsen was much with them and taught the boys their lessons. Rahel could not take her eyes from his hands. They had been her pride and she envied the bleached manicurist at the Hotel Métropole where her father had gone every Friday afternoon. Now there was hair on the knuckles and the nails were broken. The servants

89

left and the cook marched off with one of her mother's furs, threatening obscurely. Instead of milk-bottles, they found small parcels of excrement on the door-step.

One evening Madame Jakobsen told the children to lay their coats and jackets on her bed. She took her sewing-box, with its gold-leaf monogram, threaded the needle, and emptied on her lap a bundle of yellow stars. Later Annie came over; she too was wearing a star, where the emblem had been on her school blazer. The two girls held each other and stood in the rank garden sobbing. That was the last time they met.

In January a man came to see her father. He had an unkempt beard and said that the end of the community was imminent. The lists of those to be deported were ready at the Brussels *Kommandatur*. It was the time foretold, the time of the wolves which is night. It had been like that during the pogroms. God's will was strange; but Akibah of ever-blessed memory and other learned Masters have said that so long as we cannot fathom His inscrutable purpose, we may strive. The children must be saved. Some were being taken in by Christian families, others might be smuggled into convent schools. The man gave them the name of Dr. de Veeld. Only two weeks later, Monsieur Jakobsen and his eldest son were summoned to the Gestapo for the customary chat.

When de Veeld appeared, Rahel knew she would not see her father again. But the worst agony was his refusal to look at her. He held her in a smothering embrace. She felt the spasms racking his body and his tears covered her face. But he kept his head averted. Now she was no longer certain she could remember the colour of his eyes. Only that he had said her name over and over, Rahel, Rahel, in a voice not his own.

"But why me? Why not David? It's he that matters. I don't know whether I believe in God. Not any more. But we used to light the candles and say the prayers for the dead. Only a man is allowed to lead those prayers, to intone them in God's house. Even if I live and have children, they cannot carry my father's name. It will be death all over again. Why not hide David? If only you knew him; he's like my father."

I urged that her mother and the boy might be safe; he was too young to be alone. She pressed her hands to her temples, as if she were trying to see in the wide darkness.

"If de Veeld had asked mother, it *would* have been David. I'm sure of that. But my father cared for me more than for either of my brothers. It's a queer, ugly thing to say. But he made no secret of it. He had a wild temper. Sometimes he shouted at Jacob so loud that the glass decanter shook in the dining-room cupboard. And when David sulked, father hit him. He never touched me. I used to scream in my crib at bed-time. He would swoop down and bundle me off to his study before mother or my governess could interfere. If Jacob or David ruffled the papers on his desk, he would glare and scold. But he let me rummage where I wanted and gave me his cigar-box to open. When I failed algebra, mother wanted me to stay in Brussels and work with a tutor during the summer holidays. But father absconded with me on a business trip to London; he bought me a red hand-bag and we took a boat-ride down the Thames. He sent me away because he loved me best."

We had come to the high gate with its chain lock. She gripped the staves and her body was stiff with protest. Then she leaned forward, hardly breathing. She seemed to hear, in the blacked-out landscape, a distant, terrible sound. It cut through her like an unseen shaft and she let go: "Now they are taking the children. They are going to send David to those places. I hate God. I hate God."

I had intruded on an ancient, pitiless dialogue. All prayer is indictment.

Her body went slack and she allowed me to put my arms around her. A great lightness whipped through my nerves. Purge me with hyssop, and I shall be clean. It was a verse we heard often during morning chapel at Choalten (the fifty-first Psalm being a favourite text). I did not know what hyssop was.

I imagined it to be a leaf tasting like holly. It was a secret herb to burn out fear and the things in us that are muddied.

Gathered to me, that slight, mutinous form, and the liveness of her hair against my hand, were like a sudden harvest. It was not I who had scurried for cover like a wet rat or dirtied myself in fright. Holding her in that tawdry strip of garden, I broke from my own shadow.

I blurted out to her brazen assurances of life. If the Germans won, which I thought likely, there would be peace; they would allow us to go home. If not, they would have neither the strength nor occasion to carry out their plans. Our panic was breeding insane fancies. Germany was the land of Schiller and Beethoven; it spoke the language of Rilke: "Remember what was imputed to the Germans here, in Belgium, during the First World War. It turned out to be a grisly fable. They did *not* go around cutting off people's hands. We must get a hold of ourselves. Your mother and David are probably safe. You shall see your whole family again. You will live to recall these things like an evil dream. They pass."

She pulled away from me, denying: "They're dead. I know they're dead. I can't bear to know it. But I do."

"You'll make yourself mad, Rahel. You're imagining hideous things that may never happen. Your father had warning; he must have sent your mother and the little boy into hiding. The Germans can't be everywhere. You and I are alive and safe."

We act love in a worn similitude. I wanted to find a way of my own. Instead, I drew her near and laboured to enmesh her hand. I said the old words, hating those who had used them before. To me, who had never spoken them, they were new as morning. Even that is a cliché.

"If I had not met you only a few hours ago, I would say I am in love with you. I know that I will say it very soon. And that it changes everything. For both of us, if you will allow it. If you will not laugh or explain that we have empty stomachs and are light-headed. Don't say that this is happening because there's no one else we can look to in this lost hole. I would have found you anywhere."

Rahel considered me with an odd, ironic sweetness: "Yes; I think you will live. I want you to. You must promise to stay hidden or to make them let you go."

Even in that instant, with her lips pressed to mine, I sensed that the core of her yielding was hard and watchful. But nothing mattered. I exulted. I groped my way to my room, as agile and sharp-honed as a man part-drunk. As I sat down on the bed, my hand brushed against a piece of paper, folded into a minute square. I opened it and pried loose a corner of the drapes to let in the grey dim of the night. The lettering was spiky and ceremonious: "I pray you, *cher ami*, do not get involved with that little person. I don't sleep. I have been concerned over you. Probably you do not know. Indeed, I feel certain you don't. Her hair is not really blonde. It never was. She is merely a dirty little Jewess."

6

The next afternoon I found the note in my pocket. I took an enraged step. I thought I had torn up the vile scribble. But it clung like a burr.

Naturally I knew. That was the point of her being at St. Aubain. From it sprang the marvel, the sheer marvel, of her presence. But being a part of the story she so urgently told and of circumstances I could not separate from her vivid charm, Rahel's Jewishness had seemed to me no less impalpable or exotic than the diamond dust on Samuel Haagen's lapel.

Now that it confronted me in the malignant awareness of an outsider, the fact took on a more unpleasing savour. It obtruded with the subtle rawness of a fever sore.

My contact with Jews had been sparse. The Fairfield Club

had no Jewish members. There were, I believe, five or six at Choalten, but the only one in my field of vision was a wet, pudgy boy. He was rumoured to be under analysis. I did not know what this signified, but inevitably the word and his appearance conjured up the thought of indelicate bottles on a hospital trolley. The lore of my crowd at Harvard held that Jewish girls were both easy and difficult. Easy, because they took a "mature" view; difficult, because they made of it what we called, scornfully, a "production". I acquired no direct evidence on the matter.

Yet as a group, bristling and coherent, the Jews did force themselves on my consciousness. No one can engage in literary studies without being made cognizant of their seducer's gift for language and their ironic devotion to the abstract. The Jew makes of language a place. He is not really at home in it (how could he be, lacking that tenebrous, immemorial complicity with the stone, leaf and ash of a land, which give to speech its precedent, unspoken meaning?). But he masters it with the nonchalant adroitness of a privileged guest; he chucks it knowingly under the chin.

In my Renaissance seminar there was one of these gipsy conquistadors. He was a heavy young man with an actor's mouth. At one instant he was all edge; in the next, humility hung on him like a banner. He had been educated in half a dozen countries ("Herr Hitler, you know") and spoke English with flair; but he retained a sugary intonation, part French part German. I detested the fluent acrobatics of his mind. He made a vaunt of being a free-lance, a bird of passage skimming from centre to centre. But he loved Harvard with covert design and hoped to be kept on. When last I heard of him, he was pursuing a vague career in journalism and writing his academic patrons arrogant, melancholy letters.

Like most people, I found that Jews left me uncomfortable; I parted from them as from a stiff chair. When I began working on my edition of Garnier's *La Juive*, I recognized in the soaring lament of Israel, in the desolation of those whom the Assyrian had ravaged and blinded, the crux of my discomfort. By their unending misery, the Jews have put mankind in the wrong. Their presence is reproach.

That I should have fallen in love with Rahel Jakobsen was part of the logic of bad dreams which harried me since Angers. But the fact was unassailable. It braced like hope and the flash of rain on a summer's night.

Light of heart, I provoked occasions of sentiment. I tried to pierce the Saturn's ring of quiet and miasma behind which the deranged and the obsessed travel their blind orbit. One of the senior inhabitants of St. Aubain was a small, bulky personage with a grey lion's mane. Ordinarily, he was housed in sour repose. But twice or three times a day, he leaped out of his seat into a prize-fighter's stance and weaved and jabbed in a close bout with the air or his own shadow. I met him in the parlour, his guard up and his left hook slashing. I countered his posture and we sparred. Into his eyes came a sudden focus of reason and delight. He nicked me smartly on the nose. My own jabs went wide; through the drowse of his mind, the body remembered its cunning. But the blaze of nerve passed from him as abruptly as it came. In the instant in which his arms fell, I landed a blow on his chest. He stared, uncomprehending. He retained no glint of awareness of our game, but swore at me with loud, recondite obscenity.

Madame Alice had stolen upon us. She gave a frosty laugh and pulled me away.

"You do make a fool of yourself, don't you, *cher ami*? How can someone of your breeding humour this scruffy old beggar? He never bathes."

I rubbed my nose.

"You have a kind, genteel spirit. I knew that when I first laid eyes on you. But you are indiscriminate. One must guard oneself and keep up proprieties. Particularly in a place like this. There is so little tone here. I say it for your own good."

Her hand fluttered on my sleeve.

I was too buoyant for astuteness: "I got your note, Madame Alice."

The Owl took a distant air: "My note?"

"I am new here and I value your interest. Believe me. But it was not kindly put. As you say, these are thin times. We must show to one another grace of heart." The phrase had come to me during the night's content; I took pride in it: "Grace of heart, Madame. It's the only way."

She regarded me with mournful hauteur: "I require no lessons in grace. I wonder whether you would have been of our circle in Bruges. I fear not. You could not see my garden for dahlias, and in the autumn there were fresh chrysanthemums on my table each morning. No, Monsieur, you are indelicate."

The reproof was acid but her fingers tightened on my arm. And when she spoke again, her voice had a cracked, anxious note: "I told you we must stick together. Are you blind? Don't you realize that this place is thick with Jews? They're holding us as hostages, to deceive the Germans. They're weaving behind our backs, like spiders. I suppose you think de Veeld is one of us?" She grinned harshly: "He's not. His real name is Grünfeld. He was an abortionist in Liège. I can tell the chosen people a mile off. It's the way they walk." She instructed me in a fervent whisper: "They lean forward on their toes. They belong nowhere so the ground is hot under their feet."

I was startled; it was an observation I had made in my own casual experience.

The Owl sensed her vantage: "You know I'm right, *mon cher*. You and I are in their net. But we shall turn the tables. I have friends in high places. I have told them about you. There is no need for you to know who I am. Perhaps you have guessed." Her breath was on my cheek: "Promise, my dear, promise you will stay away from that little slut. She's not your kind. Promise me."

I disengaged gently. The fact that Rahel and I were linked,

even in so withered a mind, made my passion less fragile, less premature. From Madame Alice's galled reproach it took substance. I was grateful.

"You must bear with my follies." And I kissed her parchment hand.

"Ah. You won't promise. That baggage has seduced you. Your tastes are vulgar, Monsieur. I shall have the organdie dress sent home."

"Let's be friends, Madame Alice. I know I shall need your help and counsel."

But she ruffled away in anger and I felt too much heart's ease to care. Had I been cooler and less involved in the novel wealth of my feelings, I might have thought twice about the proposal Dr. de Veeld made to us that night, in his terse, indifferent manner. He remarked that those who felt inclined might contrive a sketch, or a few scenes from a play for the staff and guests: "It will take our minds off our stomachs." Rahel clapped her hands at the idea. But I still wonder at the impertinence which made us choose *Le Misanthrope*. The play and its inevitable casting fixed the constellation of enmity.

To our frayed circumstance, rehearsals brought a tang of the old, free habits. We gave of ourselves with spendthrift urgency. The realness of our stage, with its three chairs and spread of canvas in a corner of the refectory, created in St. Aubain that unbarred skylight by which prisoners reckon their chances. For a few hours each day we lived our masks.

Dr. de Veeld's assistant played Alceste. An insurgent liver had yellowed his skin and kept him out of war and conscript labour. He had a heavy Flemish temper and entered the rôle with admirable gloom. I, of course, was Philinte. Rahel cast me for the part the first evening we met to read the play. She saw in me the sweet reason of the trimmer. I winced at the aptness of her choice. Madame Alice accepted the guise of Arsinoé with such lofty calm that I wondered whether she had previously reconnoitred the piece.

97

Rahel took Célimène in glittering tow. She lavished on our meagre enterprise the prodigality and quicksilver of her being. She hoisted sail and pennon and rode before our petty wind as if all the west were open. In contempt of anguish, of what she knew of her family and foresaw, unblinking, of her own end, the girl assumed, during the hours of our mime, the pert, flickering lightness of Molière's lady. But because our actual condition hovered close, revoking us to fear like a muster on a prison morning, Rahel found in the marquise what I take to be the secret key. Under the sparkling insolence, amid the fusillade of whimsy, ran a current of feverish alarm. When she moved, even in minuet, it was like a leaf driven.

In our nervous, exhilarating game, we crossed the line between acting and daylight. The marquise says in rhymed couplets "Be my confident", and I took Rahel at her word. But the trust she gave me, the intimacy in which I shared her thin hopes and nightmare dread, had its purpose. At first I was too unguardedly happy to notice. As we knelt near each other, daubing white paint on our canvas backdrop, the Owl leaned over to hiss lugubrious warning: "*Mon pauvre ami*, don't you realize she's using you?" That Madame Alice should be jealous, and I the object of her wilted ardours, seemed doubly appropriate— to her imaginings and to the play. I evaded gallantly: "Ah, Madame, you are right. But how may I resist the charms of the marquise? She is using us all."

But the force of her suggestion grew. In those March days, liberated from the gritty shyness which had so often severed me from other human beings, I gathered, as with arms outflung, Rahel's presence, her touch, her evening welcome. Late winter has its sudden gold. But I also discovered her tenacious design. Perhaps that is too cool a word. She obeyed desperate impulse.

Rahel carried inside her, like still water, the boding of death. A grain of tender malice persuaded her that I would survive. She never doubted that I would be released from St. Aubain and come home to America. She resolved to store in me her only possession. I was to remember. That was her unspoken, vehement demand. I was to remember every detail: the house, Uncle Samuel's diamonds, the last holiday at Le Zoote, the Chinese mirror in the foyer, Aunt Ruth's arrival in her ominous shoes, the Friday manicure at the Métropole, the high-flown loves of Annie Landau. Everything. Every detail.

No repetition was superfluous; no insistence too blunt. Each conversation, between cues or when we met at work in the kitchen garden, narrowed to a hawk's circle; after a few moments, Rahel would descend on a stretch of memory and pin me to familiar ground. She made of my listening a sanctuary. In it, she and her family were to have their only survivance. There would be no other trace. She used me, with utter intent, against the monstrous oblivion unleashed on her kind. Outside St. Aubain were those who had sworn that no one would even recall the names of the dead, that their sum would be ash. The Jakobsens, the Haagens, the Landaus would have neither graves nor the fitful resurrection men are allowed in the remembrance of their children. Dust had more future.

Against this enormity Rahel set her will, as if the flare of a match could rebuke night. The Jakobsens would have their ghostly life in our house in Belmont, in cousin Peyton's library on Mt. Auburn street, in the Somerset Club. She did not realize that living Jews have small welcome in these places. But for the span of my recollection, Rahel and those near her would escape the obscene silence of massacre. One by one she lit in me the candles for her dead.

Proud scruple compelled her to offer an exchange. In retrospect, it seems obvious. At the time, I had only obscure, painful intimations. In lucid moments, I hated myself for cajoling from her tragic need a hint of recompense. I knew the bargain was contemptible. But Rahel had jarred me into blind want. I whispered to her that we were safe, that there lay before us a spacious chance of life. I lied to myself about her motive and took the pressing, unashamed gift of her past as if it was a spray of lilac tendered in flirtation.

I listened closely. I exhibited the virtuoso precision of a scholar. I repeated what she told me and echoed her merest allusion. I did not make a single error in recalling the tangled lineage of her Galician uncles. When she forgot the name of Annie Landau's governess, I reminded her. Rahel was grateful and left her hand in mine.

7

Only the violent did not attend. Guests and staff crowded the hall. Excitement simmered during the afternoon and at supper there had been spurts of sultry impatience. The tow-headed boy let loose his unsteady rein and charged about the tables telling nasty jokes. He climbed on a chair and grimaced till the tears came. De Veeld had difficulty calming him. But now he perched on the crowded bench, his face pale with delight. The florid gentleman wore the defiant remnants of evening dress and stared at the curtain, as if to exclude from his urbane content the maimed and bewildered who sat beside him. The cook and the two serving maids had come from their lair. They commandeered the sofa and whispered loudly. The gaunt creature who rationed out tea looked around like a queen of cards, her eye unblinking; she knew that everyone in the room depended on her cold grace. The gardener leaned at the rear; he had put on a clean collar and moved his neck in irked pride. Now and again he winked—not at anyone in particular—but at the entire company, gathered in the curtained, steaming room in the complicity of common magic.

An arm-chair had been reserved in the front row. De Veeld reclined as if the blade of his ironic alertness had snapped closed. He drew in small puffs on one of the Player's from his dwindling store.

Our means were ragged. A Bunsen burner, masked with red paper, served for a flambeau. The kitchen table wobbled under imagined brocade. We had patched our costumes of what eccentric or reversible clothing lay at hand and must have looked like a shabby-genteel family driven out of its house by a night fire. The sole object of unfeigned grandeur was a Victorian ink-stand. On it, a mother-of-pearl Psyche spread desolate arms over an enamelled Eros. Madame Alice had brought it to St. Aubain from some improbable corner of her past. She added it to our scarecrow furnishings with high disdain. It proclaimed a world inaccessible to our vulgarities.

But despite our starved props, the play held. In St. Aubain no one thought it absurd that a man should find society a bruising riddle, that he would try to lash its cobwebs from his face and strive for exit. The rage of Alceste played on the raw, broken nerves of our audience like intimate memories. When I spoke my worldly sermon, warning the Misanthrope that total sincerity could shade into madness, a heavy, electric wave broke over the benches. Behind my stiff make-up and the hiss of the burner, I could hear the boy breathing hard.

But it was the scene between Célimène and Arsinoé, the flash of feather and claw in Act III, which brought our performance to a pitch, and made disaster inevitable.

Madame Alice rustled on to the stage in a froth of black. She had pinned to her grey, unruly hair a cone of tissue paper. Her silhouette stole before her like a smooth bat, its wings mantled.

She opened on a note of syrupy venom: "Madame, I am here as a friend. I have come because friendship has its duties." She dropped the word *friendship* from the edge of her lips, giving it the acid whisper of steam. Recounting to Célimène the censorious gossip of the town, each item a small crystal of venom, Madame Alice seemed to uncoil. Her shadow bulked over the marquise in thick, happy gloom: "Ah, my dear, how firmly I laboured to defend your honour, your reputation and good name. But there are things one *cannot* overlook!" She ended her tirade on a cracked chime, and the lust of condescension shone on her rouged cheeks.

Rahel soared against her. She shook from the ruffles of her light, coquet dress the brown stench of the night bird. She riposted fiercely, but in the easy vein of a duellist sure of his ground. She repeated in exact, mocking counterpoint Arsinoé's pledge of amity, of unblemished kindness, and pirouetted into an irreverent curtsy.

The elegant gentleman began applauding, but held back in the nervous silence.

Madame Alice stood rigid; the blaze of virtuous reproof mounted in her bones. She grew with anger, and her features took on a weird, beaked sharpness: "You make a vaunt of your years! Am I so much the older of us two? Am I so ancient and despised?"

The arc of hatred flared between them. Rahel carried her youth unsheathed. Madame Alice sought to parry its cruel strokes. But under the menacing pavane with which she circled the stage pierced the fallen nakedness of the old.

She cried out in envy: "Is it your virtue, Madame, which doth draw such admiration from the town?"

But Rahel kept at her throat, gay and sharp-toothed as a lynx:

> *I pray you, Madame, let the gallants court,*
> *And we shall note what charms in you are sought.*

Arsinoé gripped the ink-stand. A gust of violence went through her. In a second she would hurl the murderous thing. De Veeld sat upright, and the Boxer half sprang from his place. I was paralysed by the near leap of madness.

But Madame Alice pulled herself tight. Her heavy lids closed. She cast a spell of silence, and the air went flat and stifling as in the still centre of a tropical storm. When she spoke, a breath of anguished but restored consciousness passed over the hall.

Her tone was soft and deadly: "No more. We go too far. I should already have taken leave, were it not that my carriage has been slow."

I shall never forget how that haggard, outraged woman pronounced *carriage*. She made it glitter with the lights of pride. It bore her away, past the box-hedges of a rococo garden, four Spanish pacers prancing.

As Rahel glided from the stage, in uneasy triumph, the audience rose at us. The boy screeched and the cook stamped her drowsy legs. De Veeld turned to his patients and waved them down, but the excited murmurs continued. Nothing in the rest of the play came near the savage glitter of that moment.

When the curtain fell, Rahel stood behind the canvas flap. She passed her hands over her face in a puzzled gesture, as if to wipe away the stain of Madame Alice's fury. When I touched her, she said, "I'm afraid."

De Veeld beckoned and padded ahead, conspiratorial. We trailed behind, still in our costumes. There were cups around the blue-shaded lamp and he had laid out a fresh cigarette on his blotter. He poured coffee, sour-thin and only a demi-tasse, and said it had been a fine performance. Did we realize how racked a man must be to invent such laughter? And because the thought was trite, he puckered into a shy smile. At that moment the kitchen-harpy entered, her mien torn between pride and remonstrance. She set down a covered dish. De Veeld made a large gesture over it, half sacrament, half conjurer's flourish. He whisked off the napkin. Cake.

Small, flattened at the edges, and with only one almond in its inviolate centre; but cake. De Veeld's assistant belched gently and bent forward. I was shamed by my own avid delight. "Our last egg powder," murmured the magician. "A silly waste," said the kitchen-maid. But I saw crumbs and a glint of icing on her fingers.

De Veeld plucked the almond and presented it to Rahel: "Madame la Marquise. . . ." I could taste its burnt brown. Then

he divided and was unfair only to himself. I tried small, linger-
ing bites, but was suddenly ravenous. I was scouring the plate
before I realized that everyone else had stopped eating. Madame
Alice had risen, gaunt and armoured: "Thank you for this
charming feast, *mon cher* de Veeld. But I am a little fatigued.
You will excuse me, I know. As Mademoiselle here has so
eloquently pointed out, I am an old woman. Bed-time for me.
Though God knows, I don't sleep."

"But Madame Alice, your cake . . . you haven't touched it!"
We were out of our depths.

"Ah, the cake. How kind of you. But I don't care very much
for sweets. A few pralines now and again, for the children, you
know, and a *boule Mozart*, oh ever so rarely, when we used to
go to Vienna. But otherwise, no."

The corners of her lips were moist, and she spoke in a frail
tone, as if to obscure an indelicate hurt. She looked at the
untouched slice, savouring the bitter edge of conquest: "I know
it will not be left over." We drank gall and stared at our plates.
Then she turned and slid away, dropping a general "good
night," like an ironic, twilit fanfare over a won field.

I followed Rahel to her room and ached to find it so bare.
"No pictures?"

"We had very few. Father hated being photographed. He
said that those who make a portrait of us steal a tiny piece of
our souls. I don't really know what he meant."

"I think I do."

"But there is this." She took from her night-table a tall menu
with Gothic lettering: *Le Duc de Bourgogne*, Bruges. From the
paté du chef down to the brandied cherries wound a garland of
signatures. Her father at the top, in a heavy surge: Nathanael
Emil Jakobsen. Then her brother. Near the bottom came Annie
Landau, the A round and wavy.

"We lunched there on my seventeenth birthday. There were
fifteen of us. Look at the way David signs, with that kite-tail at
the end. Do you know the Duc de Bourgogne?"

"Yes. It's the only place where the chocolate mousse is really black."

We sat on the bed.

"It's the first time for me."

"For me too."

"I don't believe you."

"I don't mean it in the same way. But it's true. This is the first time that matters."

"Have there been many?"

"No."

"Were they beautiful? I'm sure they were prettier than I."

"No."

"You won't hurt me, will you?"

"Not for the world."

She rose and stretched her hands towards me. I held them fast. Did she say "Remember"? I think not. Her purpose was desperate but not gross.

"Please don't look. It's such a silly costume. I made this of cardboard and one of de Veeld's handkerchiefs." She undid her bodice. "I wish I was wearing something beautiful. Mother has a slip bordered with dark blue lace. She said I could wear it at my wedding."

Her breasts were small and high. The dizziness of the wood came on me. For a moment, I was certain it was Rahel, that it was into her skin they had rubbed the cinders. Then my mind cleared. I saw her supple, guarded body.

"Please hold me. I'm cold."

My hands were in her back. We shivered like the gently drunk. Then she closed her eyes.

Much later, nearly at the grey of morning, she began laughing. I lifted her warm cheek. "It's Annie. She said the first time was like a saddle-sore. She had read it in a book. It isn't." And she laughed till I drew the blanket over us.

8

They came four days later. The bark of the dogs woke me, and going down to breakfast I saw the two black cars in the yard.

They made us sit in the parlour in a wide, still circle. One of them leaned against the door. There was no savagery in his face; he had a puffed skin and swollen lids, like a factory-worker at mid-afternoon, when the light tires and there is precise, tedious labour in hand. I had seen such faces in my cousin's foundry in Waltham.

He did not shout at us, but announced that if anyone wished to leave the room and use the toilet down the hall, they would have to ask permission. At this we grew obeisant as children. Each one seemed to fold inward, attending, in embarrassed isolation, to the sting of his bowels. The gentleman gave a stifled sigh; even at this early hour, and at sudden alarm, he had inserted a handkerchief in the breast-pocket of his pyjamas.

After a spell, one of the elderly women got up; holding her green house-robe she shuffled to the guard. She whispered. He made her repeat her request out loud and shook his head. She retreated to her seat, bewildered, and kept her eyes on the man's face in abject alertness. Then he nodded and she hurried past. Later he summoned the Boxer: "Stop flailing about. You may go and relieve yourself." The old prowler flushed: "But I don't need to." "I think you do," said the guard patiently.

We did not dare look at each other, but sat utterly divided, each cowering in his own sweat. When the officer came, they made us get up and sit down again. But the boy had wet his trousers and the leather chair, so they stood him in the corner with his forehead to the wall. The officer expressed regret at our inconvenience; he hoped we were being looked after. If everyone behaved sensibly, we would soon be allowed to go back to our rest. He pronounced the word with nostalgic malice, as if it came from a child's primer. It was really up to us. They had thought for some time that the home was being used to shelter Jews and subversives. They had been very patient, but now the matter had to be cleared up. It was for our own benefit. He only hoped Dr. de Veeld would take a reasonable view. If not. . . .

In the corner the boy sagged; another faint trickle ran over his shoe. The guard stole up behind him, gripped his flaxen hair and thrust him against the wall, twice, not very hard. When the boy sat down, his teeth clapped.

Without lifting my head, I caught a glimpse of Rahel. April was in the garden and she was staring out. Against the lit window, her features were delicately drawn and calm. She was fully dressed, as if she had been ready before us. I cried to her with every nerve, but she did not hear.

It seemed to me as if a day had come and gone under the glass bell. My mouth was hot. But perhaps it was less than an hour. Then the other sound. From somewhere in the covert of the house, a thin, blurred cry, a cellar murmur, and the cry again. Rahel shut her eyes and the woman in the house-robe scraped her hands convulsively on the arm of the sofa. The guard yelled at her: "Quiet. Stop that stupid noise." But he himself was whistling and banging his heel against the door. I realized that the dogs had stopped barking.

They dragged de Veeld through the room, slowly, forcing us to look. His mouth was a dark hole, and his right hand hung from his sleeve, the nails bleeding. As they slid him by the arms, down the corridor and towards the stairs, one of his sandals came loose. De Veeld always wore sandals; he said his feet were rheumatic.

This time the officer's tone grated. His tie was twisted and there were stains on his silver-edged lapel. He disliked having to do this kind of thing. It was no pleasure; he hoped we realized that. But de Veeld had been stubborn and a liar. It was a doctor's job to care for the sick, not to hide runaways and Jews. The *Kommandatur* had allowed St. Aubain special rations.

None of the buildings had been requisitioned: "We have treated you like a hospital. We shall know better in future." He hoped the patients would prove more reasonable than the doctor. The guard laughed. The officer said he would wait in de Veeld's office for anything we chose to tell him. But he was a busy man. He would wait fifteen minutes. If no one came forward, if those who were hiding under false colours did not have the decency to give themselves up, he would clear the house. And in the garden were the dogs.

I do not remember how many minutes passed. I knew her prim step so well there was no need to look up. I could have acted—sprung from my chair and throttled her, or gone to the officer myself to warn him that Madame Alice was a hysteric, that everything she said was a crazy lie. I could have convinced him that it was I they were looking for, that there was no one else. All the resolute, sane gestures of day-dreams or remorse are possible; but they hover on the edge of an instant. I sat paralysed. In the second before the needle enters or the mask comes down, the brain races through a vile litany: let it happen to someone else, to anyone, even to someone close to me. But not to me. So the reel unwound, hideous and expected.

The officer returned and examined our huddled group. He called, not loud: "Rahel Jakobsen." She rose. "Get your things. *Sie kommen mit uns.*"

He left and she began moving towards the door. Then she looked me full in the face.

Theology tells of a moment, intolerable to reason, when Judgment will be over and the gate of Hell will close on the final damned, not for unnumbered millions of years, but for motionless eternity. As the light fades upwards, the damned will look at God's back in terrible forgiveness.

I tried to read in her still face a shadow of fear or of relief. But there was only this terrible mercy. Then she was gone, and soon the cars drove out of the yard.

I flung myself into her naked room. The menu was on the

bed. I knew there would be a message, a word of parting or of hope. I scanned the signatures wildly, turned it over and searched the corners. There was nothing. Nothing whatever.

9

I have been back to St. Aubain.

It was a very hot day and my mother stared with irritation at the sweat-blisters on the chauffeur's neck. He was encased in his grey uniform, and though the front-seat was large, his elbow brushed continuously against the three-tiered package which towered beside him.

We crossed new bridges and the houses were freshly painted. My mother shifted on the leather arm-rest and tapped her alligator travelling-case. She regarded the venture with prickly scorn; it was the kind of complication she associated with the infrequent appearance in Belmont of unemployed French Canadians or refugee doctors from central Europe. She had allowed the excursion only because it fell easily between the Memlings of Bruges and the tulips of Delft.

Mother's first cousin was in the State Department. Through his influence and the good offices of the Swedish Red Cross, I had been extricated from St. Aubain before the war ended. "Why do you want to go back to that place, Bunny? We had enough trouble getting you out." Europe was an old enemy; Uncle Winslow, her younger brother, had gone there in the thirties. After idling in Paris and Dublin, he had come home to a hasty marriage. As we crossed the canal, mother said: "I do wish the chauffeur wouldn't perspire so."

The home had been enlarged. There were white roses in the hedge, and parasols and croquet mallets on the lawn. Where the kitchen garden had been, they had added a solarium. Behind the screened windows, I saw shadows at ping-pong. "This is more pleasant than I expected," allowed my mother, "but then you do exaggerate."

The senior psychiatrist received us in his office. He frowned thoughtfully when I asked about de Veeld. He had died in a camp. It was a wretched business. But he had never quite understood why de Veeld had dabbled in clandestine politics. A doctor's prime duty lay with his patients. Though it had no red cross painted on its roof, a mental home was precisely like any other hospital, neutral ground. So far as he knew, the Germans had been scrupulously correct. It was de Veeld who brought on the difficulties. "I myself happened to be in Switzerland during the war, working in Dr. Jung's clinic." He pointed to a signed photograph on his large desk. No, he had no record of what had befallen most of the patients. In 1944, the Germans used St. Aubain as a field-hospital. Then the Americans took over. "It was in dilapidated shape when I first came. But we feel we've done quite well. We're planning a separate wing for electro-therapy."

Dr. Brunel was so pink and serene that I grew flustered. I tried to explain what it had been like and why our chauffeur had carried in, and unwrapped on the hall table, a large cake. Mother had insisted on a frosting of stars and lilies, but I wanted him to know why it was a mocha-layer cake and why the walnuts were so important. I tangled in my own words.

"You're getting all flushed, Bunny. Please relax. I'm sure the doctor isn't interested in the unfortunate details. What we want to do is get the cake to a cool place."

Dr. Brunel dimpled and said it was a charming gift. Of course, most of the patients were on a low-calorie diet: "In the old days, psychiatrists were careless about that. We know now how vital slimness is to the ego. In a way, rationing was a blessing in disguise." But the cake and the thought behind it would be fully appreciated. If we had a moment to spare, he would be happy to show us around: "When the Americans

110

left, they presented us with a bowling-alley. It's in the basement. Let's start there."

I excused myself. There were a few places I wanted to revisit on my own. Dr. Brunel winked: "You are a sentimentalist, I see." "He gets overwrought," said mother. But I slipped away.

There were muslin drapes in the parlour and the old sofa was gone. A young woman in a starched white uniform was arranging flowers and putting lotto-cards on the tables.

I went upstairs, sick with loneliness and desire. I prayed, in absurd hope, that she would be in her room, that I would hear her voice once more, and touch my face to her dark hair. She would turn from the window as I entered and laugh low to see me so wild and happy. I would cry out to her that since she had left me, my life was ash.

I walked towards her room and stopped. The corridor was unchanged except for the new, beige wall-paper. But I no longer remembered which door it was. I hurried up and down the hall; I counted. But it was no use; I simply did not remember. The doors stared at me vacant. I heard myself whimper like a lost dog. Then panic and wretchedness swept over me. I gripped the radiator pipes and tried to call. But bile came up in my throat. I vomited and stood over my dirt helpless. Luncheon music sounded from the garden.

I came down the stairs, still dizzy. The cake had been cut and was being handed out on flowered plates. My mother was deep in conversation, her hand on another lady's arm. She turned to me, the small lines around her chin crinkling with pleasure: "Come over here, Bunny. I've met someone who remembers all about you. She's told me the sweetest things. What a small boy you still were."

I stood rooted. Madame Alice had grown plump and there was a blue sheen in her hair. She set down her plate and billowed towards me in a profuse print dress: "*Cher ami!* How lovely to see you! How perfectly lovely. I knew you would come back one day to visit me. I said it to Dr. Brunel. He never contradicts;

he's a dear. And why did you never tell me about your *maman*? *Elle est charmante!* Come here, you wicked young man. I've got something for you."

She held before her a parcel festooned with ribbon. Through the cellophane, I saw the ink-stand, and desperate Psyche, her wings outflung in never-ending sorrow.

"It's for you, *mon petit*, in remembrance."

Perhaps I uttered a cry. Everyone in the room suddenly looked up and mother called my name sharply. Then I began running.

Sweet Mars

1

The amorist loves London in June. Your true lover is a November man. When the air is grey to the breath. And the armada of houses tugs at its mooring, as if the winter gust of the sea were in the streets, and the salt spray in the stripped gardens. Nowhere else in the world, in the smoke-light of a winter evening, does the harvest lie so close-packed, of the past, of the present hurry of mind and footstep. The rain draws its curtain in Talbot Close; the undersea lights go on in Cheyne Walk; and the wind carries the savour of the Smithfield stalls across the dark of St. Bartholomew's. At the quick edge of night, the gulls pass indifferent from the spars of the ships riding off Limehouse quay to the inland masts of the steeples. The trains run empty between Whitechapel and Holborn, and the City is left to its bells. If you want to hear silence breathe, stop in Princess and Poultry Yard after the last jobber has gone home.

Or to his club. London is a city against women. Full of burrows down which foxes vanish. But there are chinks in the curtains on Brook Street and St. James's, and on a November evening the lights make a dim, golden stain in the wet fog, as if someone had spilled a Barsac on to a grey rug. Which simile begins our story.

A Barsac would have been unlikely at the C. Rather a hock for eight shillings. It had once been a club of some lustre. New members were shown Palmerston's chair and a brace of silver-mounted shoe-brushes presented by Kipling. But the C. had been damaged in the blitz and funds were lacking to rebuild the top floor or replace the cut-glass chandeliers in the smoking-room. Dust had bitten deep, and the lift had moods. Older members, reluctant to affront the stairs, along whose worn banister Swinburne was said to have rubbed his cat's paw, had to be extricated fairly regularly by means of a stepladder kept in the porter's glass cage.

To stay afloat, the C. had opened its doors widely at the end of the war. Men were taken in who would not normally have been considered. It sufficed to have held a commission in an acceptable branch of the service (and the net was cast wide to include the Royal Catering Corps), and to be able to pay the admission fee of twenty-five guineas. Thinking they would want to stay in touch, that they might want a place in which to drink in the old way—bottoms up, chin-chin, here's to you, boy—a crowd of younger men had joined. They wore their suits like tunics and whistled in the urinals. Frequently the bar ran out of whisky, and the Library Committee had to remind junior members that the *Church Times* was not intended primarily for sanitary uses.

In 1949, the C. had enough of a surplus to replace the charred wainscotting in the billiard room with a pastel motif. But strangely, a smell of ash and burnt plaster lingered in odd corners of the house.

Soon the younger men drifted out of war and into the morass of life, to Croydon, to Sevenoaks, to the modern flat and the children come too soon. The club sank back into its torpor, and on most winter evenings, when he would gaze from his perch in the chill entrance foyer towards the darting shimmer of the sitting-room fire, Pritchard, the head-porter, would know, unthinking, whose legs protruded out of the hollow of the chairs. F., a colonel from the *other* war, the real war, D.S.O. at Mons, and a collector of Arthur Symons first editions; T. Raisley (*not* Nicholas, his younger brother, whom Pritchard had seen as a boy, in the summer before Passchendaele); S.R., a City man, a Jew, but who had captained the Brigade of Guards golf team; Geoffrey Carr, who had done the first north face on the Pico Verde, and then lost his right leg in a car smash; and Ted Hobhouse, a sodden, unkempt brute of a man, a novelist

116

botched, now a critic who wrote with a broken bottle—twice asked to resign from the club for having insulted other members and relieved himself in the umbrella stand, but readmitted for the growl of his wit. And Pritchard would set his feet delicately against the guard of his small electric fire, and doze off to the chime of the clock, far off in the dim of the stairs.

But not on the third Tuesday of the month. Having attached the notice in its copper-plate script, *Reserved for Private Party*, to the knob of the smoking-room door, Pritchard would return to his perch, alert, or relieve the Desert Fathers of their duffle-coats and scarves as they came in out of the cold. Ten or a dozen ex-officers who had known each other during the war. Who gathered, once a month between October and May, to dine with mock ceremony and drink a toast to the accompaniment of a private limerick. Sometimes they sang, loud or embarrassed behind the muffling door. When they left, suddenly distant from each other, to flag a taxi or catch the last tube at Green Park, Pritchard would see them out. If there was glass broken, there might be a pound note from Major Reeve.

Reeve was secretary and master spirit. Pritchard had always supposed that the Desert Fathers were his invention. But Reeve denied it ("This was Gerald Maune's idea; Gerald thought of it. I'm only the sod who collects the dues and worries about breakage. Maune likes to talk about the war, you know. Misses it"). Reeve was a tall man with spare, exact motions. He wore his hair long, flung back, and his face had a carved elegance, the shadows in the right place, the mouth agile. He had tawny eyes and the habit of looking away, into private laughter, when challenged. There seemed to be between him and Maune a companionship so intense, so joined at the root, that Pritchard could hardly imagine the one without the other.

It had been that way at school. Maune had come to Brackens terrified. He was strong and easy at games, but small of stature. He was found out as having three older sisters who giggled and a commanding mother, who appeared at unpredictable intervals

117

and walked up and down the courtyard talking to the House-master in a fierce whisper. For some occult reason—Gerald never forgot the fact, but its tangled, sadistic motive escaped him—he came to be called Chloë. When the pack was after him, it would shout "Chloë, Chloë" in a wild treble which could still make him sweat when he thought of it.

Reeve was house prefect and unpopular for his abrupt, jeer-ing manner. He was thought too clever by half, but played rugger with nervy grace. Maune marvelled at his serenity and worshipped. One morning, after a night's fracas, someone hav-ing strung all the chamber-pots to a clothes-line and pulled them past the Master's bedroom window, the lower school was marshalled on the rugger field and made to run the cinder track in shorts. Maune had a toothache and had lain hot and shivering much of the night. It was drizzling and the sudden cold stung his bowels. He tried to put on a brisk canter but started falling behind. He was nauseated to the bone. A prefect came behind the small boys, riding herd on a bicycle. It was Reeve. Maune looked back, sickened and out of breath. For an instant, he saw Reeve's face come alight with a strange, covert tenderness, and the eyes were fixed on his as if to hold him steady. Then he stumbled and passed out.

Reeve had come to see him in the infirmary. He had enclosed Maune's wrist in his supple fingers and left a small book, with a dark-blue cover and gilt spine. "You will find some jolly stuff in there." It was an edition of Macaulay's *Lays*, and Maune had it with him still, fifteen years later, in his kit in the Libyan desert.

The story of how Captain Maune lost and recovered that kit under the fire of German mortars during the evacuation of Tobruk, was known to all the Desert Fathers. When drunk or coaxed, Gerald would retell it with increasing embellishment. Half a mile out of the burning city, he discovered he had left his bed-roll behind. Though mines were going up with an evil thud, he threaded his way back to the cellar where he had been quartered. He extricated the bulky roll from dust and fallen girders. He was only part-way across open ground when a German patrol nosed out of the blazing rubble. He lunged into a desperate, crouching sprint. At that moment the roll of toilet-paper jammed in his kit came loose and trailed behind. Instead of shooting, the Germans doubled over with laughter and shouted encouragement. The company of Greenjackets who were covering the retreat, looked up from their gunsights to see what was going on. They too began laughing. It was only when he lurched, choking and exhausted, into a fox-hole, that Gerald saw fluttering behind him, like a chevalier's pennon defiant to the wind, the long trail of paper. That night, in the shelter of the half-tracks at Wadi Haraph, he unpacked his kit and made certain the Macaulay was safe.

After his release from the school infirmary, Maune sought out Reeve. They grew inseparable. Reeve's parents had parted under circumstances the boy depicted as mysterious and sordid. Soon he spent most of his holidays at Maune's house in Richmond. The three girls pecked around him like demure herons, and Mrs. Maune was enchanted that her "nervous little man" had made so handsome a friend. One August they went sailing off the Norfolk coast. Their sloop ran on to a sand-bar and the sea hammered at it in an ugly, yellow froth. Maune never forgot how Reeve turned to him and said, clear into the wind, "If we drown here they'll never find our bodies," or the pulse of delight that rose in him when he heard the words. Reeve won an exhibition to Magdalen, and Gerald followed a year later. One October night, in 1938, they stood together in the garden, looking back at the still tower, its blackness heavier than the night air. Unthinking, they clasped hands and swore they would take life at the full. And Reeve said, *"C'est le partage de minuit."*

But that pressure of the real, which Gerald strove for, came crass and unbidden.

He had gone hiking in the Cotswolds and came to a pub near Long Compton drenched. The girl who worked at the bar took him upstairs and told him to strip off his clothes so she could hang them by the kitchen grate. Her voice had a warm edge and Gerald felt his skin prickle. After a few minutes she came back into the room, dark and loud with the lash of rain. She was carrying a pot of tea and a jigger of rum. Gerald huddled on the bed, wrapped in a towel and sweater. She asked him whether he had caught a chill and poured the tea. The abrupt heat made him shiver. "It's a rub you'll be needing." Her hands passed over him like her voice, heavy and near. She found the nerve of him and the darkness of the room hammered at his throat. He turned and touched her breast. "You're a quick one, aren't you? There. There now. Don't be mussing my hair. It's your first time, isn't it?" And she had laughed with a low, queer warmth, seeing him so wild.

They had not met the next morning and when the letter came, two months later, Gerald stared at the signature perplexed. "You've got me into a spot of trouble. Bad trouble. I'll meet you in front of the Lamb and Flag tomorrow at six. I hope you're keeping well. Very sincerely. Ina."

She was waiting, her mouth sullen. She was damned sorry. But there it was. More than a month gone. No, there could be no mistake. She had been to see a doctor in Birmingham. She had told her aunt. He would like her aunt. She was a real sport. She had said to Ina, "don't fret so, duck, he'll do the right and true thing by you."

They were walking through the Parks in the dead smell of early winter. "You will do the right thing, won't you love?" She slipped her arm into his. "I'm not a tart, you know." He was choking with fear and misery. She taunted softly: "You were a bit livelier that night, weren't you love?" Oh she knew all about what the nice young ladies at Oxford did when accidents happened. Had it taken care of in London or abroad. Have an abortion? Not bloody likely. It made her retch to think of it. Let some filthy brute of a Jew-doctor put his hands on her? There'd be none of that, Mr. Maune. Yes, she had seen his name (a sweet name she thought it was) and college when he registered at the pub. The sooner they got settled the better. He didn't want everyone to know she was in a family way, did he? She'd have to hurry along now. "I'll meet you here again next Friday. It's my afternoon off. And we can have a spot of dinner together. Take me to the George, won't you. I hear they do a smashing dinner. Be a sweet, won't you love." At the gate of the Parks she kissed his cheek and breathed in his ear: "Maybe we go somewhere. Afterwards. It doesn't matter. Not now, love. Ina Maune. I think it sounds super." He tore away, appalled.

The next days were a nightmare. His whole world lay splintered. The years of school, the proud hopes, the compact with life made under Magdalen tower, all gone to nothing, to this hideous, vulgar trap. The thought of thrusting such a creature on his mother was unbearable. He loathed the sight of her, the rough, wet smell of her hair, the dabs of rouge on her chafed skin. He would kill himself. He would settle his account at Blackwell's, write his tutor a note suggesting he found university work too stiff, and do away with himself. The notion of living with the woman and her child in some rathole was far worse.

After taking his decision, Gerald felt at peace. It was morning and he walked through Christ Church meadows strangely elated. The sky was immensely high and the ground sang with frost. A white mist came off the river, and the early sun pierced through. A thrush stood in the wet grass and rose away from Gerald in a slow arc. He exulted at the silence and the mounting fire of the light. Then he strode home and fell into an utter sleep.

But when he woke, the foul stupidity of the thing closed on him. Every nerve cried out that there must be a way, an escape. He would simply leave, drop out of life, change his name, hover about in hiding until the whole sordid affair had blown over. He would go far away. The name Valparaiso trotted through his brain in an absurd jig. Other men had got women pregnant and not had their lives smashed. It was hideously unfair. Other men slept with girls as if they were cracking nuts. It had been his first time. Why had he stopped at the place, why had he let her come into the room when he was naked and feverish? Maune turned desperately in his cage. Then he went to Merton chapel, knelt and touched the altar rail. Sixteen times. The number was his talisman. After the sixteenth time he would wake, and the whole thing would pass from him like a vile dream. He performed the rite with furtive passion. But he came into the light helpless.

Friday came inexorable, and he hurried to see Reeve. Reeve glanced up when he burst into the room: "Crikey. Do you have malaria? You look like the mother of death. Have a drink." Gerald poured out his misery; even to himself he stank of fear and lack of sleep. His legs were shaking. Reeve surged out of his cavernous chair and stood over him: "You nit! You little nit! You've really gone and buggered yourself, haven't you. Jesus, how could you be so bloody stupid! Just look at you." Gerald remembered a whipping he had had in school. Reeve's contempt made his eyes water. Then, as quickly as it had blazed, Reeve's charring anger dropped. He spoke very quietly: "You're not going to see the girl. You're not to go anywhere near her. Do you hear me? I will. She's probably lying. She's trying to put a bite on you. Crummy tart. I'll give her five pounds and tell her we'll call the police if she shows her face again."

"What if she's telling the truth?"

"Just leave it to me, boy. I know where she can get fixed up."

An obscure, bewildering pain stirred in Gerald. But he was too grateful, too burnt out to say anything. Reeve left him crumpled on the sofa, asleep.

When he awoke, the shilling had dropped in the gas-meter and the air was bitter cold. But Gerald's body was full of sweat, and hearing the tower bells strike seven across the dark, chill quad, he cried out in the empty room. The minutes crept over his skin and he shivered till he thought he would break. Loud as his own pulse he heard Reeve's footsteps, across the echoing flagstones and up the unlit stairs. For a maddening instant, Reeve seemed to pause on the landing, then he entered. Gerald rose at him, his teeth on edge.

"You gave me a start. I thought you'd gone home. You look a fearful mess. And there's no need to stare at me like a lunatic. You can get off your knees now. She's gone. Lost and gone for ever." And he hummed the tune under his breath.

Gerald was choking for air: "What happened? What did she say? For God's sake, tell me."

Reeve crouched by the grate and brought the flame to a slow, exact hiss: "I tell you, everything's all right. Forget about it."

"But I want to know. Is she going to have something done to her? Did she want to see me?"

Reeve turned, breaking the used match between his nails: "You worry too much. That's your trouble, Maune. You worry too much." And he came near: "You asked me to take care of it, didn't you? You came in here shaking so bad I thought you were going to puke your guts out all over the bloody rug. You were on your knees for help. Well it's over and done with. No fuss no muss no babies born. Fair enough? Now leave off, boy, I'm telling you, just leave off."

Gerald caught a queer note in Reeve's voice, as of envy. Then relief welled up in him, uncontrollable: "My God, Reeve. I'm so grateful." He grasped Reeve's hand: "You don't know what this was doing to me. You can't know. I was going to kill myself." He gave a loud, sad laugh. "I was going to kill myself. I'd got a note ready for old Tyson. And one for you. You don't believe me, do you? But I swear it's true. I couldn't face it. Kill myself. Can you imagine? But I'm never going to be such an idiot again, never." He began dancing through the room. "Let's get pissed. Let's get so bloody pissed they'll have to float us home!"

"You're on," said Reeve.

They sat at the Trout, dangling their feet over the parapet. They had had six pints and it was near closing time. Reeve blew the foam from the rim of his glass. He was outwardly sober, but curiously alert, as if there were voices in the river. Gerald was swaying in a soft stupor; happiness had loosened his nerves. Between draughts, he gulped the cold taste of the night and the rank scent of river-grass. Part of him was drifting into thick sleep, but still he laughed to find the gates of life open again.

Then he heard Reeve asking, as from far off: "Do you know there's going to be a war? You don't believe that gaff about Munich, do you? There's going to be a war, Maune, and I'm going down to London to see about a commission."

"Are you?" said Gerald, and then with bleary tenderness, "Are you really? I say. That's rather grand."

Reeve shook him by the shoulder: "You're blind as a newt. You're absolutely stinko. We'd better get a move on."

Gerald laboured to his feet and saw the world was on a tilt: "Is there really going to be a war? I think you're just trying to confuse me. That's what you're trying to do. Confuse me." He stumbled gently against the table.

Above the churn of the weir, the peacocks shrilled their naked cry. Reeve was standing on top of the parapet and calling to the loud tumble of water: "I tell you, boy, there's going to be a war. Any day now. And mark my word: it's going to be the biggest and best war ever!"

2

It was. The finest hour. Full of the ceremony of death. But also a high holiday for the living. Away from school and spinach. A time in the half-light, when one's flabby shadow took on the airs of a hawk, and one mattered. All of a sudden, to oneself and to others in the complicity of the mad game. When women said yes, in covert places, because men carried about them, like a sweet, unnerving scent, the claims of death. Because pity makes one's bowels hot. A time when strangers locked arms and sang in a common sweat. When chartered accountants grew sunburnt and grocery clerks looked tersely at the moon. A vacation from paper towels and blocked drains, from Sunday afternoons at Woking, and the office party. Some met Dante on a roof-top in Russell Square, coming out of the voice of the smoke; others saw the glow of a cigarette in the shadow of a hangar, and a girl in a tunic saying, keep well. A time when a man found himself asked and able to do things he had never dreamt of, in intricate, murderous machines, behind antennae and code-books, under the white hammer of the Libyan sun, or in the cockpit of the sea. A time when he could do them in bed, and found a friend in the mirror. Sweet Mars. It was not like the one before, with its rats, and gas-stench, and eternity of mud. If you weren't a civilian blitzed or shovelled into the camps, if you could stay out of Burma or the Murmansk convoys, it was a good war. And hard to come home from.

Major Duncan Reeve had a distinguished record in Intelligence, first in the Mediterranean, later as a liaison specialist in France. He was awarded the D.S.O. in 1944. War's end found him in Hamburg. He tried to settle in England, but drifted about loathing its grey virtue. In 1946, he decamped to America on the strength of a vague contract as publisher's reader and the chance of writing as a stringer for the *Yorkshire Post* (he had met editors and correspondents in the corps, and they had told him there was always an opening for a man with a quick eye).

He bought a third-hand Pontiac, a typewriter in a red plastic case, and *The Leaves of Grass*. Then he set out across America. In the evenings, and off the road during the heat of the day, under a sky flung wide and wasteful as it never is over England, Reeve wrote a novel. About the war and the comely dead. He was uncertain whether it should be acrid or mournful; but racing down the green canyon to Salt Lake City, he hit on a title: *Chariot over Jordan*. He scrawled it across page one of the manuscript and blew smoke into the air, exultant. Sometimes he said it to himself out loud.

It was in a dinette, on the South Side in Chicago, that the girl heard him and turned smiling. She had wide, pale features, sumptuous black eyes, and wore the honeycomb of her hair cut close like a boy. She was dressed in a man's shirt and tailored slacks. The heavy Mexican brooch at her throat caught the light, and Reeve laughed at her cigarette holder, with its long lacquered stem. She was like something out of an Aztec version of the flappers.

"I am Vivianne" (she insisted on the French spelling, though she came from the east side of New York), "who are you?"

They went to the Beehive and ate pizza, sauntered through Lincoln Park under the yellow eyes of the cops, and stood by the lake shore watching the red pulse of light over the steel mills in Gary.

She made her eyes wide: "I don't like the name Duncan. It tastes like a crunchy-bar. I want you to be called Siegfried Sassoon." She sang it out across the lake: "Siegfried. Siegfried. Isn't it a gorgeous name? It makes me all cold inside. *Ici.*"

"I entirely agree," said Duncan, "I can't understand why I haven't changed before."

"But you are a hero, aren't you?"

"I certainly am. All Sassoons are heroes. Come home and I'll show you my citations."

"Kiss me before we go."

"No, not here." It was their first quarrel.

She said she was an art student and had done modelling. She was writing a poem in heroic couplets entitled "The Lesbian's Lament" and recited Baudelaire at breakfast. Maman came from an old French family, but had married a bum who had drunk himself to death in Scranton, Pennsylvania. Duncan listened to

126

her tales with complete disbelief and total trust. Whatever Vivianne said, had in it the truth of the moment. Her imagination could not lie; she wore it naked.

They drove westward and he finished the novel in a motel near Lake Tahoe. She dared him to go in the icy water and stood on the bank, suddenly frightened, as the cold knocked the wind out of him. Then back east to make the round of the publishers and pick up some money lecturing about the war. Sometimes they would drive the night through and spend the whole day in a hotel room. Vivianne registered as Siegfried and Siegmund Sassoon, or as Mr. and Mrs. John Katz, of St. Agnes, Hampstead. ("I am sure that was his real name. Who ever heard of anyone called Keats?") When Reeve lectured—his best performance dealt with Arnheim: "Was it Espionage that Betrayed our Gallant Force?"—Vivianne sat in the last row, behind the Gorgon ladies with their blue-tinted hair, waited for moments of high pathos, and made ribald faces. "You are a fraud, aren't you, *chéri*? I hope you didn't put that crap in the novel."

They got married the day *Chariot over Jordan* was accepted. They drove across the bridge to Hudson County, and Vivianne insisted on paying the Judge of the Peace an extra ten dollars so they could take along his rubber plant.

"Did you see what was embroidered on the antimacassar?" asked Vivianne. "May Jesus bless Your first caress And make each kiss A fount of bliss. Isn't it beautiful? Isn't it just beautiful?"

Reeve laughed, but she was crying, and when he bent close to stroke her golden boy's hair, she gave him a startled, remote look. He felt suddenly very tired, and instead of pushing on to open country, they decided to spend the night in Trenton.

The hotel had a sour smell and the neon signs slashed through the Venetian blinds. Chewing the soggy toast in the cafeteria, Duncan thought with abrupt hunger: "I must get back to Europe and a piece of real bread." Vivianne said she wanted to go upstairs, "but give me half an hour. And don't put on that

127

silly, supercilious smile. This is our wedding night. It's different. Or hadn't you noticed?"

She was sitting on the bed in a thing lacy and ephemeral.

"Let's have a drink," said Reeve, "I'll ring the bellhop and tell him to bring us some whisky and a bucket of ice."

"No. I don't want anyone else to come into the room. Not tonight. Please."

For a long time, he stood by the window.

"Won't you come to bed?"

The flashes of neon cut across the dank wall-paper.

"Look Vi, don't be mad at me. It's just no good here. The place is too god-damned ugly. Just look at it. Just look out the window. I've never seen anything so bloody awful. Look at those signs. They keep the bloody things on all night. Serutan. Spells nature's backwards. It does. Nature's backwards. My God, it does! I'm sorry sweet, but I'm going to have that drink if it's the last thing I do."

She was very still until the bellhop came. Then she leaped up on the bed, kicked her heels at the ceiling and cried out: "May Jesus bless Your first caress And make each kiss A fount of bliss." Louder and louder.

"Stop it, Vi, stop it! This isn't a god-damned whore-house. It just smells like one. Now stop it!"

But she wouldn't, and after the Negro boy retreated, with a frightened grin, Reeve slapped her hard.

They took an apartment in Greenwich Village. When the basement laundromat started up, the floor shook and Vivianne declaimed Empson on earthquakes. Reeve taught French in night school, tried to sell articles about his travels in America, and hammered at a second novel. But even as he wrote, he knew the thing was strangely inert. The edge of feeling had gone out of his work; it wore thin over the exits and alarms of his daily life.

A year passed.

His marriage seemed to move from quarrel to quarrel like an

electric arc. But the reconciliations were worse, great gusts of pardon and intimacy which left him hollow. Vivianne had gone back to modelling and came home frayed and restless from the long hours of tense poise under the lights. The good times came before dawn, in the unsteady silence of the Square, when they perched on the rim of the fountain, too drowsy to play on each other's nerves.

Chariot over Jordan was published in the fall. For the first ten days, Reeve bought all the newspapers and magazines unashamed. There was no mention of the book. He and Vivianne circled each other in silence. She knew his hurt and it made her raw, as if he were sitting in the room with no clothes on. A week later she came quickly up the stairs: "There's a notice in the *Village Voice*."

"Have you read it?"

She lied: "No," and handed him the paper. He took it and turned to the window. He read it to himself, then aloud, in a dead tone: "This first novel, by an English author now living in the Village, sets out with high intentions. Using the war in the desert as an allegory of the larger struggle between reality and dreams, between the quest for solitude and the demands of love, Duncan Reeve asks that we judge his work by high standards. Unfortunately, he has bitten off more than he can chew. There are patches of lyric prose which betray the obvious influence of Malcolm Lowry, and a few flashes of sardonic wit. But as a whole, the book is pretentious and lifeless. It gives the impression of being the work of an old man, gone sour, rather than of a first novel by a young writer who still has everything to learn about his trade."

For a time Reeve said nothing, but stared at the paper as if it were a living thing. Then, folding it carefully and throwing it away, he remarked, as to himself: "I haven't read Malcolm Lowry."

She watched him pour the drinks and started towards the light-switch.

"No. I don't want any light. Not just yet."

So they sat in the heavy dark and drank.

"Poor sweet. Perhaps you are an old man. Perhaps that's what's happened to us. They've found us out. The chariot isn't swinging low. It's left the station. *Pauvre vieux*."

It was her own voice, but she did not remember saying it. He got up and she thought she could hear his fists close. He picked up the pages of manuscript on his desk and tore the sheet that was in the typewriter. Then he went to the bathroom. She heard the toilet flush and gurgle mournfully, and flush again. His misery made her spine cold. When he came into the room, she said in a stage whisper: "I'm Hedda Gabler. I've destroyed my child." Reeve bent over her, his breath stale with whisky: "You're not Hedda Gabler. You're just a bitch."

A few weeks later, Reeve asked Vivianne to come home with him to England. When she said "No," he knew she was right. Being modern, they decided to part friends. Vivianne was keeping the apartment and Reeve asked her to forward the mail. They went for a cup of coffee in the corner drugstore.

"I hope things work out for you, Duncan. You know that's true, don't you?"

He nodded.

"And you'll think of me sometimes. I wasn't a bitch all the time, was I? You remember when you said I was your golden boy. But golden lads and girls all must Like chimney-sweepers, come to dust. Those are marvellous lines, aren't they? They're so marvellous I don't think I can bear it. Who wrote them?"

"Siegfried Sassoon."

He stared down at his knuckles. He felt her hand on his shoulder.

"Look Vi, shouldn't we give it one more chance? Just one. I mean. . . ."

Then she was gone.

Reeve stood at the railing as the liner entered Southampton

Water in the grey of a March evening. He was chilled to the bone, and wondered why England was the coldest place on earth, colder than Labrador or Queen Maud land in the white antarctic, cold with a thousand years of damp. The ship moved slowly between the anti-submarine booms, the radar-towers and camouflaged caissons. Reeve could see the broad gashes burnt by the raids in the Southampton waterfront. The houses stood small and huddled against the cold green of the hills. A plume of soot drifted over the water and across the pale bar of twilight. Reeve felt trapped. Why is the place so ugly, so cowed, like a cat gone rotten in the teeth? What am I doing here? Panic swept over him, and the impulse to return to America at once, as soon as he could beg or pilfer the passage money. Three years since the war ended. And you'd think the place had been blitzed last night. My God, we love our wounds.

Reeve flinched at the bored, clipped tones of the customs officials in the wet gloom of the shed. He went out in the street, with its charred walls and rain-puddles, aching for a drink. He had forgotten about licensing hours and found the pubs closed. He took refuge from the downpour in the parlour of a small hotel. An odour of floor-wax and gas-burners, of aspidistra and bacon rind enveloped him. Reeve asked whether he could have a meal. The girl's voice was triumphant with denial: "I'm very sorry, Sir, but we don't do suppers. Not at *this* hour." "Do you know of any other place around here?" "I'm sure I don't." She waited in austere scorn. "How about a pot of tea?" "I'll see if the kettle's on. We don't usually do teas, not after supper, you know." "My God," said Reeve under his breath, and stared with utmost concentration at the framed lithograph of King George V, *Our Sailor King*. The bearded personage behind whom vague dreadnoughts were firing at a blur of sea, stared back. "And a pack of Player's, if you would Miss." Now Reeve remembered that matches had to be extracted from a box marked *Dr. Barnardo's Homes. Thank You.* He fumbled in his pocket and found nothing but an American dime. The girl's stony eye watched him as he turned away and crushed the unlit cigarette in his palm.

The need to hear a living voice rose in him like a dizzy spell. He had lost touch with Maune. They had met in Alexandria during the war, and Reeve recalled, with distaste, Gerald's unguarded enchantment, the candid, nearly vulgar pleasure he seemed to take of life and the new intimacies war had brought. They had drifted apart. But now Reeve experienced an intense longing for their old trust. A childish relief went through him when he found the name in the directory: Gerald Maune, 12 Hillcrest Lane, London, S.E.19. He remembered to push Button A, but was utterly, absurdly taken aback to hear a woman's voice. "Mrs. Maune speaking. Who is it? Who is it, please?" Reeve said his name and the voice took on a brisk cheeriness. "How lovely to hear from you! What a surprise this will be for Gerald. He speaks of you often. I feel I know a lot about you. I'm Sheila Maune. Yes, we've been married two years. Let me see, more actually, twenty-six months. We did send you an announcement. I know we did. Didn't it catch up with you?"

Now Reeve remembered, vaguely, the little envelope and rustle of silk paper which he had glanced at, amid a pile of letters and circulars, when driving through Phoenix, Arizona, or was it at the San Francisco post-office?

"Where are you? When will you be in London? How marvellous! You must come and look us up right away. Gerald is out, but I know how anxious he'll be to see you. How about Monday night? No, wait half a second. Make it Tuesday, could you? Do you know how to get out here? It isn't too bad once you get on the right tube. It's going to be grand meeting you after hearing so much about you. Just wait till I tell Gerald."

Reeve had a few minutes to spare before the London train. He walked out of the station to look at the harbour. He could see nothing, only the black downpour, and far away, the blink of a lighthouse. He buttoned his collar, but the cold lurked inside.

3

The Maune flat was brisk Scandinavian. Two Braque prints on the living-room wall, a Danish travel-poster showing a family of improbable ducklings halting traffic in a crowded street, Vivaldi's *Four Seasons* on the record-player, and the Penguins on the book-shelf. Momentarily, Reeve toyed with the idea that he was back in the Village, or visiting friends on Morningside Heights. But as Sheila set down the sherry and tired biscuits, he knew he was home.

She was small in stature but strong-boned, with rather heavy features. He was struck by a low, rough-edged quality in her voice. Gerald had gotten heavier, and the years in the desert seemed to have reddened his skin. He had a boisterous laugh which Reeve had not known before, and a trick of drumming on the table with his knuckles. He was delighted to find Reeve again, and they stood clasping hands like victorious schoolboys.

"We'd given you up for lost, you know. Gone for a Burton."

"Only America."

"Same thing, I imagine. Gone for ever. It's grand having you back. You *are* back for good now, aren't you? You won't run out on the old place again, will you?"

"I don't know. I've just come back. Give a chap a breather. I've lost touch."

"A fair number of people are thinking of going to America," said Sheila, "more of a chance all around. It must be odd coming back. Don't you find things drab here, and a bit mildewed? You know what I mean, as if they'd been in the wash too often and had never had a proper airing."

"One does feel that a bit. I keep looking for lights to switch on. As if the whole place were having a power cut. It's grey."

Gerald laughed and turned on a large Chinese lamp in the corner.

"We got it at Primavera's," said Sheila, "one of our first

splurges." She poured more sherry: "Don't you think you'll miss it? America, I mean. We're terribly run down. It's beginning to smell like a rooming-house we used to go to in Eastbourne. They'd never let daylight in. Not since Prince Albert passed by. It was a funny smell, lavender and cabbage."

"You do exaggerate," said Gerald, looking at her with plump ease.

"There *are* things I'm going to miss. Fiercely. The size. I don't see how you can put it in words really. But America is so big. There's enough sky for everybody. We had a spot of sun this morning, you remember? I was walking in Green Park and looked up. Suddenly I had the queerest feeling, that I shouldn't look too long, that I was taking more than my fair share. As if they'd rationed the whole place. A shilling's worth of sun, a coupon's worth of lawn, half a pint of sea-air from Ramsgate, and oranges for the kiddies. And no cheating. Coming up from Southampton, I kept staring at the houses. They'd all shrunk. There's so much room in America. Here I'd worry about gunning the car; I might go right over the edge." He sipped the flat sherry, and memory came on him with ironic force: "I was driving north from Boston last October. The sky was so blue it made your eyes blink, and I turned into a stretch of wood. The maple-leaves were red; not rust-red, but deep flame-red. The air had a tang of wood and sea in it as if the world had just begun. Every time I took a breath it was like neat whisky. I had to stop the car. It made my bones sing. And the way American women walk. You know, as if they had a wind at their back."

"We have thick ankles," said Sheila, "it keeps us steady when the deck rolls. Seriously, what made you come back? It all sounds too marvellous."

Reeve knew she was jabbing: "Oh lots of reasons. I don't really know, I suppose. But it isn't all peaches and cream. There are things you can't have in America."

"Draft Bass," said Gerald.

They laughed, but Sheila kept alert, trying to mark the real drift. When Reeve began telling them, she leaned forward immensely interested.

"You see, I got married over there. And it didn't work out." He told them the story, or parts of it. In an odd way, he found it fascinating. He hadn't, in fact, heard it before. His voice gave it a peculiar distance. "I dare say that's the real reason I came home."

After due silence, Gerald said: "Have another drink." He said it a little too loud, and flushed.

Sheila vanished. Then they heard her call: "Supper's on." As Reeve passed into the small dining-room, Gerald went over to the lamp and switched it off.

"I've done all the talking. What about you?" Reeve listened intently. Failure had left him raw. But already, as he set them in the apology and composure of the past tense, America and the ruin of his marriage seemed to grow less urgent. Listening to Gerald, and cutting the potatoes which Sheila served from a bone-china tureen, Reeve felt ground under his feet. Gerald's words, which meant either more or less than was actually being said, were deeply familiar. He recognized their exact pitch. He had found the flat candour of American speech marvellously exciting; but he settled back, as after a hard run, into the old semi-tones.

"I work on *The Real Estate Chronicle*. We're the biggest in the trade, you know. We've got a new press in south London that can turn out colour stuff as good as any in France. I write for the paper on and off. But my job's in the research department. Looking into the history of properties, trying to forecast trends, advising clients about local regulations and county councils. I'm on the road a good deal. As much, in fact, as I'm in the office. That's how I met Sheila. There was a block of freeholds up for auction on the edge of the New Forest, and I went down to have a look. Sheila was on holiday in Lynd-hurst."

"Cursing myself, the rain, and the treacle. Gerald came into the hotel bar and dropped his papers all over the floor. He looked so stuffy and angry that I couldn't help laughing. He was down on all fours and looked up as if he was going to bite my head off. Then he came over and we met."

Gerald had poured the wine. "God bless," said Reeve. It was tame claret but made him feel easy.

"It's not a line of work I'd ever thought about. I don't suppose I ever thought about anything very practical while the war was on. I happened to be in Tunis when the show ended, trying to get a mob of prisoners sorted out. Chap I knew in the Quartermaster's office—older man—asked me what I was going to do after I got out of the army. I told him I hadn't made any plans. I must have imagined the old war would never end. Go on until they put me on retirement pay. He told me to look him up when I got back to London. I didn't at first. I couldn't get used to things. You know, ordinary things."

Reeve noticed Sheila's hand poised, very still, on the stem of her glass.

"I tried to get a rest at home, but Mother drove me crazy. Every time I tried to tell her anything, about how it had been and why I was all wound up and queer inside, she looked at me with an air of frantic interest, and I knew she wasn't listening to a word. There was no one I could talk to. And I had all sorts of wild dreams."

"What about?" Sheila had gone to the kitchen, and had turned on the water with a loud spurt.

"You know, things I'd seen or heard chaps talking about. One in particular. It kept coming back. It must have been a few miles outside Benghazi. An eighty-eight had hit one of our tanks full-on, and the bloody thing caught fire. I don't suppose I was more than a hundred yards away. I heard the man in charge—I knew who it was, Welshman with blue eyes that didn't quite match—telling the crew, very steadily, not to panic, that they'd climb out of the turret. But the shell must have bent or fused the hinges. They couldn't get it open, and the rear port-hole was full of burning oil. So he called for help, saying please, all calm. We tried to get near, but the sand was going black under the heat, and the plates were buckling. So they began screaming. Like men trying to scream to other men. They were roasting alive, by inches. Then their voices changed. They sounded like a pack of little boys. You remember, Reeve, when they used to yell at me, Chloë, Chloë! Something like that. All high and crazy. But that wasn't the worst. Near the very end, when they were burning alive in there, knowing we were just outside and couldn't help, their voices stopped being human. It was like hearing a bird, when it's on the ground crippled, and the fox is near. Just an insane whine. And in the middle of it, the Welsh chap saying please, gentle like, as if he didn't mean to inconvenience. I kept dreaming about those voices, and hearing them in odd places. When the tea-kettle started up or a train whistled."

Even across the table and the steamy smell of greens, Reeve caught the edge of fear and sweat. But Maune took up, relaxed, as if a precarious rite had been performed.

"I larked about for a bit. Dropped in on chaps I'd known in the regiment. I sailed on the Broads for a week with a chap from Bomber Command. Mad as a hatter. Wanted me to go into business with him, running a special kind of holiday tour for Yanks: 'Come and see the ruins of Coventry. Week-end in Rotterdam. Look at what you've been missing.' Then I got tired of drifting, and went to see the man in London. He turned out to be rather a big fish, and got me a berth on the *Chronicle*. I met Sheila on one of my first trips out of the office. I was lucky. I don't think it would have worked without her. I was still pretty jumpy. We had our ups and downs, I can tell you."

"He almost didn't show up at the wedding."

"I would have dragged him there," said Reeve.

"God knows where you were! You never wrote a line. Not even condolences."

Reeve lied: "The announcement must have gone astray. Pony Express once you get past Chicago."

"No matter," said Gerald, "it's good to have you back. I've missed you, you old devil."

Sheila bustled: "Why don't you both make yourselves useful and get out of here. I hate having men around when I do the dishes. Anyway, if Gerald doesn't put in an appearance at the Queen's Arms, they'll start worrying. He goes there every night."

"Sheila, you know that's a lie!"

They bantered, and Gerald surged into the kitchen. Reeve heard Sheila catch her breath, and then a warm, smothered laugh.

The Queen's Arms was a Victorian pub, with cut-glass mirrors and stained panelling. Gerald ordered stout. He drank fast and the words spilled: "It's going all right, you know. On the paper, I mean. The flat was a bit of a strain, I can tell you. I'm into the bank rather more than feels comfortable. But we're starting to put aside a little. So far as taxes allow. You'll find out soon enough; they can sweat blood out of a stone. I don't suppose it's anywhere near as bad in the States. But still, we're keeping the old head out of water. Have to. Sheila wants children. She wants them very much."

"And you?"

"Oh, I don't know. Yes, I suppose I do. It'd be rather nice in a way." He laughed and shook himself like a wet hen. "But what I really want now is chaps I can talk to. Sheila's a poppet, and I don't need to tell you how fond we are of each other. You have eyes. But I often feel as if I was carrying a bloody big suitcase everywhere I go, and couldn't put it down. It's got the things inside it that made me the way I am. The things I remember happening in the war. There's no use telling anyone who hasn't been in it. They listen, all right, but they just don't hear. Not even Sheila. Am I talking rot?"

"No. I often felt that in America. They've had a war. But it's theirs. Not like ours at all."

Gerald's voice thickened: "That's exactly it, chum. And if

everyone is going to act as if it hadn't happened, as if we'd dreamt it up on a bad stomach, I'm going to start believing them. But it's a lie. A lot of spivs who don't know what it was like and don't have any use for us." His arm was on Reeve's shoulder: "Mustn't let the buggers steal a man's shadow. Look silly without it."

"Time, gentlemen, time."

"Nice thing about American bars, they don't kick you out into the rain at ten-thirty."

"Fuck 'em," offered Gerald with glad rage.

"Last round. Time, gentlemen, please."

In the cold of the street, Gerald's tone cleared: "Sheila doesn't know this. But those dreams."

"What about them?"

"They're back. On and off, for a while now. And you know, Reeve, a funny thing. I had the one, about the bloody tank burning, the night you rang from Southampton. Sheila told me when I came home. I was more pleased than I'd ever admit, you old bastard. But I woke in the middle of the night shaking. I could hear those screams as if they were in the room."

"Home with you now," said Reeve, and as he gripped Gerald by the arm he thought of the evening at the Trout, and of the golden treachery of that last summer.

4

Of Gerald's need, and of Reeve's discovery that divorce had left him lonely—it was a feeling he had never experienced before, and it jarred him—grew the Desert Fathers. Gerald had a schoolboy's pertinacity in keeping track of chums, of their whereabouts and private lives. The ease with which he conjured up, out of the anonymous vast bustle of London, a dozen friends or acquaintances happy to meet once a month and share with each other memories and contempts that were becoming unreal or embarrassing to those around them, convinced Reeve that Gerald had been a remarkably competent, popular soldier. Plainly, he had been the kind of officer who hurried leave papers and covered other men's failings of exactitude or nerve. He had found the decent word in the ugly moment and made quite the best of the crude, stylized intimacies of men at war.

At first, the Tuesday nights had an uneasy casualness, everyone acting as if they had dropped in by mere chance and had to be quickly on their way. But men who have been to public schools or spent time in an officer's mess have an instinct for ceremony. Put them together, and they will, with an unspoken self-amused art, contrive rites and forms. No one seemed to remember who first ordained that evenings should end with a toast to the Young lady from Cairo Who always carried a Biro, or the rule of the sconce, whereby whoever missed two Tuesdays in a row had to buy port for the whole table and contribute five bob to the Limbless Ex-service Men's Association. Pranks or habits of speech, which are puerile to an outsider, can bind. Hearing the smothered echo of Quinton Moore's delivery of *Lili Marlene* (with new and unofficial lyrics), Pritchard would shift happily in his seat. No women, no civilians, all was well in the world.

Nearly all the members had served in the Middle East and the desert. Several had been in Gerald's mess. Reeve, who had found work in a small publishing firm, renewed acquaintance with two former colleagues in Intelligence. Each had gone his private way; but they shared a deep, unsettling awareness of the force of memories, a covert suspicion that the ballast of their lives had shifted to the past, and that they might not find again a like tautness and intensity of being. It made them nervous like a buzz in the ear.

Brian Smith had a phrase for it: "They've gated us. They told us to go out and have a whopping rag on the town. Now they've shut us in. Welcome to the coop, chum." His own was narrow. He had married a dry, vehement girl who did modern sculpture; now there were two spiky children. Smith had joined the reserves, and had an annual fortnight's training with the Territorials. His usual air of mournful cunning brightened at the approach of summer.

Brownlee had served in the cavalry. Nothing in his elegant, soft features and prematurely silvered hair indicated that he had taken a patrol of armoured cars through the El-Quatarah depression, that they had been cut off by sand-storms and pinned down without water, and that he had led them out, half-crazed with thirst, but without the loss of a man or vehicle. Just before the war, he had married a girl somewhat older than himself and of means. He had come back to find a woman sour about the years lost and the gnawings of middle age. She strove to make up for the nights apart, but after two miscarriages there fell between the elegant, reserved man and the accusing woman a large silence. When Brownlee left the club, it was not always for home.

Moore was the only member to have been in the Brigade of Guards. Small, raffish, but gifted with a fine tenor voice and Irish lilt, he still recalled with cheery disapproval the time when he and his platoon had perched on the back of American Sherman tanks during the assault on Tunis, and had listened, appalled, to the querulous informality of exchanges between officers and enlisted men. In the Guards, a man asks leave to address an officer. But Moore was no fool. He glimpsed the merits of the other code. During the scrap in Sicily, an American company on his left had been surrounded. The ranking survivor was a Negro cook-corporal. Moore had got through to him on the wire: "Listen to me closely, corporal, and don't panic. Are you presently in contact with the enemy? Repeat: in contact?" Back came the chocolate tones: "In contact, boss? Why we's eye-ball to eye-ball!" Moore told the story with delight, against himself. He had an Irishman's lust for chaos and found peace drab. "I feel overweight." He was in advertising: "It's a trade for tarts and ponces. Any advertising man would sell you his mother. In my firm they'd deliver." Now his main pleasure was to collect wines. His need of women was furtive and occasional.

Parkins had been parachuted behind the German lines after the breakthrough at Monte Cassino. The partisan group with which he was to establish liaison had been rounded up. He himself was captured a few hours after coming down. At the Waffen-SS post, they put his head into a large vat of urine, over and over. Each time he passed out, they kicked him back alive. When he no longer stirred, they left him for dead. He had come out of the affair with a D.S.O. and a vagueness in his eyes. He was a barrister of some note, and would have thought it intolerable to make of his experience emotional or professional capital. When his growing son proclaimed that middle-aged men who reminisced about the war were retarded boy scouts, Parkins said nothing. But his memories kept their cancerous hold. He found a great calm in being, from time to time, among men who could, out of their own lives, gauge the truth and quality of his hurt. Who knew that such things had happened, and that they had had some order of logic or necessity. He was senior in the club (Father of the House), and in charge of the annual dinner.

The second took place in the winter of 1951. Inevitably, the long table, with its decanters, its silver cigar- and snuff-boxes and candle-sticks, evoked a full-dress night in a regimental mess. Parkins had come early to see that all was in place. The drapes had been drawn in front of the high windows, but he could hear the brush of wet snow against the panes. He worried the black tie in his slightly frayed wing-collar, and peered again at the printed menu (engraving had been voted too costly). The Desert Fathers. Second Annual Dinner. November 16th 1951. The health of the Society to be proposed by the Father of the House: Lt. Col. R. Parkins, D.S.O. Mr. Gerald Maune, President, will reply. *Vegetable cutlets Kiev. Boeuf braisé à l'Irlandaise* (rationing cast its shadow). But Moore had picked the wines.

Couched in its silver basket, the Château Talbot reflected the tipsy flicker of the candles.

"Evening, Smith. Come in, man, you look frozen. There's Brownlee. Close the door like a good chap, will you. Let's get started on the Fino. Hullo Simpson. I say, that's a handsome dinner jacket. I hear they're wearing them in neon blue in America. Do join us. Or do you prefer the very dry?" Parkins poured sherry and had a last quick look at the place cards.

Moore lifted the claret out of its repose and held it fondly to the light: "This is the real thing. Wasted on you chaps. Utterly wasted."

Reeve came in rubbing the chill from his knuckles, followed at once by Gerald. T. Wilson, Royal Artillery, late. "As usual," said Simpson. "Shall we sit down?" "Give the blighter half a minute." Wilson barged in apologetic. He had stepped too near a land-mine in Tobruk and carried a cane: "Awfully sorry. Came as fast as I could. Work, you know." General groan of disbelief. "Some of us do have to work for a living, you know. Don't see how the rest of you manage." He was a partner in a small brokerage firm in the City: "Fearful jam in the tube. Gets worse every winter."

They sank into their places and the club steward began serving.

It was Brian Smith who arrested the general tide of voices, clinked glass and china.

"Do you mean that, Smith?" It was Wilson, startled.

"I'm afraid so. I don't honestly suppose I'll be with you chaps a year from now."

Simpson, his knife suspended: "Hullo, what's all this about?"

"I'm getting out. Taking the family to Australia."

"Why?" Brownlee leaned forward.

"Fed up. That's all. Just plain fed up. Bloody pipes frozen. Coal shortage. Another winter like this? Not if I can help it. I'd like to live in a place where you can get really warm, through to the bone. I caught a whiff of my children the other day. I tell you, they're going mouldy."

"Come on, Smith, be serious."

"I am, Brownlee. We were sitting home last week, wondering whether we had enough shillings for the meter, trying to figure out whether there'd be anything at all, one bloody farthing, left after taxes, and all at once Claire and I looked at each other and had the same thought. Why hang on? Geoff might have an outside chance to get into a decent grammar school. Jimmy's a nice little devil, but not long on brains. Won't get near it. I don't know what's happened, but everywhere you go now, there are a million people queueing for the same spot or trying to scramble ahead of you. Haven't you noticed? You go to a restaurant, and you queue out the door. You drive to what used to be an empty stretch of beach in Devon, and you can't park within a mile of it for all the caravans and comfort stations. I tried to put Geoff's name down at Charlton. My uncle is an Old Carltoonian and it looks a decent sort of place. They're booked solid till 1965. The whole island is like a boat with too many people jammed in it. One of these days some bastard will pull out the plug, and it'll all sink."

Voices cut in, nervous or aggrieved.

"We've had a bad patch of it, I'll admit that," said Wilson, "but from where I sit, it looks as if we'd turned the corner."

"Until the next balls-up. We're awfully good at crises and girding our loins. Look at this flan. I shouldn't have thought it had come anywhere near a fresh egg. Why, the Krauts are eating better than we. And getting more of it. Right now. After the whole place was smashed into a shambles. We have a real talent for being dreary and pretending it's good for us. The old loin has been girt once too often."

"There's something in what you say. But I couldn't imagine living anywhere else. Not among foreigners. And I rather like the flan!" Simpson chewed with obstinate flourish.

Voices were still loud and at cross-purpose when Gerald

tapped his glass. Silence gathered, then a scrape and shuffle of feet.

"Gentlemen, I give you His Majesty."

"His Majesty," and Parkins, under his breath, "God bless him."

"Gentlemen, you may smoke now."

Some edged their chairs back from the table, stretching. Others strolled in the room lighting cigars. The steward put more coal on the fire, took away the wine glasses, and set down brandy snifters and small glasses for port. Moore took a pinch of snuff and let the tawny flakes lie on the back of his hand.

Gerald went to the wash-room. He had a grey, absent mien, as if he was in secret pain. Reeve had followed him.

"Anything wrong?"

"No. Nothing really." He moistened the corner of a towel and sponged his face. It shone with small beads of perspiration.

"You sure you're all right?"

"Perfectly. I had rather a set to with Sheila. And a poor night. I'm feeling a bit flogged. That's all. We'd better get back."

Maune in the chair: "The Honourable Secretary will now read the minutes of the last meeting."

Reeve did so, with customary embellishments. Resolution that Wilson be sconced passed by acclamation. His assertion that he had missed two meetings because of a business trip to America was rejected as implausible. He had been observed with a lady, not his wife, behind a potted palm in Brighton.

Wilson: "Mr. President, Sir, I protest!"

Protest not allowed. The port started around the table.

Reeve went on: "Proposed assessment for the present dinner: seventeen and six per head."

Ritual cries of "Shame!"

"Far too expensive. How much of a profit does the honourable member make on these inferior clarets?" Simpson's question was ruled out of order. Further protests, and Moore, mock-outraged: "I take a loss. A cruel loss."

"If no other honourable member has any point he wishes to raise, I will sign the minutes." Reeve placed the blotter on the page and closed the leather tome.

As Parkins got to his feet, the room grew so silent that the Desert Fathers could hear Pritchard's winter cough reverberating bleakly in the club foyer. Parkins stubbed his cigar, carefully, into the silver ash-tray by his plate; there was a nervous glow in his pale cheek: "Mr. President, Sir, I am no public speaker."

Soft denials: "Rubbish."

"Ask anyone at the Bar. That's why I settle all my cases out of court. I used to fancy myself a regular orator. Lost too many clients that way. When I got up to speak, the Judge began brushing his black cap." (*Laughter.*) "So I can promise you, Sir, that this will be brief. I don't know about other honourable members, but for myself I can say that I am very pleased that every month has a third Tuesday."

"Hear, hear," and rapping of glasses.

"I don't know that we're a frightfully bright lot . . ."

"Point of order," hissed Moore, joyously.

". . . or that we accomplish very much beyond helping Moore lay down his cellar," (*laughter*) "but I know how greatly I value the chance to be with a group of men—how should I put it?" (He seemed to cast about for his meaning, his fingers searching, and in the absence of his voice the rain was loud.) ". . . With a group of friends—I do feel the word is in order . . ."

"Hear, hear."

". . . who don't need to have things explained to them. The things that matter. Because at a time when each of us learnt what certain words meant—the old-fashioned words, the ones we had read in books but not felt in the cold of our own backs—we were in the same boat. Hanging on for dear life. But not only for that. And no one pulled the plug out, though I dare say we all wanted to more than once. And may I say, Smith, that I hope

146

you'll be with us, not only a year hence, but for many years to come. Because I just don't believe we're finished. Not yet. Not when I look around this table." (*Loud approval.*) "Sir, I take great pleasure in offering the health of the Society."

"The Society." Then fists hammering till the glasses danced and Brownlee, with a connoisseur's nod: "Nicely put, Colonel, very nicely put."

Gerald got up. His eyes sought the opposite wall, as if trying to focus on some point in the shadows. He took from his pocket, and unfolded, smoothing the ruffled edge, a front page of *The Times*. He began low, and Wilson, at the far end, cupped his ear.

"Honourable members are no doubt familiar with this object. It is the cover page of *The Times*. The only page on which there is any news." (*Laughter.*) "Known to all men who served in H.M.'s forces for diverse other properties. Particularly when on air-mail paper." (*Loud amusement.*) "There is no end of wonder to be found on this page. Miss Doris Moufflon: colonic irrigation; opens and relaxes." (*General mirth; Simpson doubled over.*) "Betty: letter lost; please write. Your Tooty." Or: "Am eighteen. Anything legal considered. Also other possibilities."

A happy roar. Gerald read on: "Entrancing black Chihuahua bitch. Fearless. A real charmer. Rabies serum available."

Moore pounded the table, his eyes watery. It was the hour of port and smouldering cigar-ash, when laughter is a conspiracy, doubly warm because it is withheld from the poor buggers who do not share the code and are slogging by in the rain outside. Only Reeve noticed the clenched whiteness in Gerald's face.

"But I wonder whether honourable members ever look to the left of the page. Bottom left, or top of the second column. Depends on how many there are. Every day of the year. Unfailing. Even Christmas Eve. Never a single day without them. Rather a lot this morning."

Brownlee had come alert; the others were leaning back,

drowsy and smoke-wreathed. Gerald read slowly, as if there was a desperate shrillness poised, ready to tear his voice at the root:

"Colmer—In memory of Jack. Lt. J. N. Colmer. Killed in action. November 16th 1942. He gave all. Per ardua. Mum and Joan.

"Forbes—In proud and loving memory of Harry Forbes. Captain, 9th Durham Light Infantry, killed near Mareth. November 16th 1941. With firmness in the right. Anne.

"Greggson—In treasured memory of our beloved only son, Pilot Officer Lawrence Greggson, Eton and King's, 12th Bomber Squadron, R.A.F. Did not return from a flight over Germany. November 16th 1944. We shall not see his like again. Mum and Priscilla.

"Hoskins—In constant remembrance of Nick. Lt. N. Hoskins, M.C., the East Yorkshire Regiment, killed near St. Fleury, November 16th 1915, aged 19. For your tomorrow he gave his today."

Simpson had ducked for his brandy. Moore kept his taut smile, but had his eyes to the ceiling, as if tracing an obscure, menacing fault. "Look here, Maune, you've made your point. Carry on, old chap, will you. Don't hammer it into the ground." It was Brownlee, softly but distinct. A shiver of embarrassment passed around the table. Gerald seemed not to hear: "Rather a special one, this:

"Londsdale—In never-dying memory of Major T. F. C. Londsdale, King's Shropshire Light Infantry, killed at the head of his battalion near Corvin, November 16th 1917. Of his son, Johnny. Lt. J. Londsdale, 5th Battalion, York and Lancaster Regiment, killed in the landings on the Normandy beaches, June 6th 1944. And of Susan, nurse at St. Mary's Royal Infirmary, Singapore, who died in enemy hands as a result of maltreatment. February 11th 1943. Why am I thus alone. B. L.

"Pitt-Neame—Raymond Pitt-Neame, Captain 3rd Fife and Forfar Yeomanry, R.A.C., reported lost in the sinking of the troopship H.M.S. *Niger* in the Indian Ocean, November 16th 1943, aged twenty-five. May God give us to see the right. Billy. Peter. Dad."

The ash on Parkins's cigar had gone cold: "*We* know. No need to tell *us*. There but for God's grace were you and I. Don't make a production of it. No one *here*'s going to forget. Bless them all."

"Quite right," Wilson spoke loud, "I think the whole thing's in damn poor taste. Morbid, if you ask me. Downright morbid." Then to the entire table, in a busy sweep: "Do you think Pritchard can turn up some whisky? Shall I ask?"

"I second that."

They were all talking fast and shrugging off the dark. Smith stabbed the fire-iron into the grate and a shower of red embers scattered. Gerald's voice came sharp as a cracked bell:

"In treasured memory of George Walker, D.F.C., reported missing after a raid on Aachen, November 16th 1944. We miss you so. Mummy. David. Lizbeth."

This time, Brownlee pushed his chair back: "I don't know what you think you're doing, Maune, but I've had my fill. I hope you'll excuse me, but I must get on home. It's late." Smith spun the stem of his glass between his palms, and made dim noises of reproof. Parkins crossed to the window: "I say, snow's stopped. Turning to rain." Reeve leaned over from his seat to touch Gerald's arm, but he felt curiously exhilarated.

Then Gerald spoke again, haltingly, into an abrupt, rebellious silence: "I won't go on. Though it doesn't seem fair. There are other names. Chap with a Y. Polish, I suppose. But there's something I wanted to say. About the lot of them. Every day of the year. All this stuff about how young they were. What rotten luck it was for them to die. Never-fading memory. Well I'm not sure. Maybe *they*'re alive. Maybe *they*'re the ones that are really living. That's what I'm trying to say. Don't look at me as if my fly was open, Brownlee. Give me half a minute, and I'll try and explain. It's something I've been thinking about a lot lately. Maybe we have it all wrong, and it's *we* who are dead. We don't smell dead, but we are. And they're having a laugh on us. A bloody great laugh."

Reeve tugged at his sleeve: "Stop it, Gerald."

"We're the ones they should have in *The Times*. Don't you see? We the living dead. In loving memory of Colonel Parkins. He was a hero, but who's got any use for heroes? They take up so much room around the house. In never-fading remembrance of Gerald Maune, Captain, 2nd Battalion, the Royal Norfolk Regiment. Looks alive. But isn't. Stone dead. Ask his wife."

His lips were still moving, but the scrape of chairs and the tangle of voices cut him off.

"Disgusting!" Simpson said it twice, fiercely. "Can't hold his liquor."

"Good night ladies, good night ladies, we're sorry to see you go," hummed Wilson, "time for the old sack."

"She was waiting by the lamp-post," Moore's tenor capped the angry, embarrassed noise.

Brownlee left quickly, and outside the door, now ajar, Pritchard hovered torn between curiosity and reserve. Parkins gave Gerald a shy tap on the shoulder: "Don't worry about it, Maune, I mean the way things have gone tonight. I am not sure, but I think I know what you meant, at least part of it. And take care of yourself, old man, will you? You look as if you could do with a bit of sun. Beastly winter. Good night, Reeve."

The room emptied in loud eddies: "Good night. Can I give you chaps a lift? Night, Reeve."

The candles burnt with a low, writhing flame. Only the red ash on the grate glowed against the silver and the cold stain of darkness. Gerald filled his glass and raised it to the guttering light: "Gentlemen, I offer a toast. To the memory of the living. May they find deliverance." He emptied it at one draught.

Reeve watched from the blackness of the window. He saw the tears, and the face of a man haunted.

5

When he received Sheila's note, couched in a feminine casual imperative, and asking when and where he might be free to lunch with her, Reeve felt a needling under the skin. He had been expecting this to happen, and had the nagging sensation of having been cast for a part in a banal yet cunning script.

Edging between the tables in a small restaurant near Covent Garden, one of the few where he would not, at every moment, be nodding to other publishers, Reeve saw that Mrs. Maune was waiting. She looked compact and faintly tarnished, her hands tight on her lap. She had no small talk that day; nearly at once her queries ached at him.

"I don't suppose you knew, but Gerald has not been well, on and off now, for almost two years. Oh, I know he looks well enough, for months at a time, but then he'll have a sudden break, as if something inside him splintered, deep down, and drove a lot of sharp bits into his nerves. I know when it happens. He starts flinching all over, wherever you touch."

She was perfunctory over the menu.

"It started when we'd only been married a few months. We were moving into our flat and were pretty hard up. They'd asked Gerald to take on a new job in the firm. He'd been doing awfully well, and they wanted him to take charge of part of the research department, to do more of the editing and look after staff. I don't remember the details. But it meant a raise, and I thought it a grand chance. Gerald hadn't been doing it a fortnight when he came down with something queer. Couldn't sleep or keep his food. The doctor found nothing actually wrong with him. Thought it might be a touch of jaundice, or something he'd picked up in Egypt. He told him to have a rest. Well, it went away the day Gerald took back his old job."

She dotted a crossed, nervous pattern on the table-cloth with the prongs of her fork.

"I don't really know Gerald very well. Odd, isn't it? But it's true. I don't mean that twaddle about human beings never getting to know one another. But because all of him that matters, deep down, that makes him stand or back away when he does, happened before we ever met. I don't know how it is in America," she looked up momentarily with a flick of malice, "but here at home, when you marry a man of Gerald's class, it's as if you were being asked to move into a house that's all furnished, that's got suits hanging in the wardrobe and cigarette boxes, and jokes you laugh at but don't quite understand. And often the phone rings, and you hear voices which sound muzzy, as if the line were bad, but they've called before, before you were ever there to listen."

The waiter interposed, but Sheila scarcely glanced at the plate.

"It's all been put together and furnished, the curtains hung and the walls stained, before a woman gets near. In school. Does anything ever happen to you after? Really happen? And at Oxford. And then in the battalion and at war. I imagine that's like being back in school, with prefects and outdoor games, and nurses in the infirmary.

"Before I met Gerald, there was only half of me. I may have looked all of one piece, but honest to God, I was only half alive. I thought that's how it would be for him. That it took two to make a whole, that it was something one built from the ground up, together. Oh, I knew everyone had their past. I suppose even I did in a small way. But I thought one would pool that and make it new, that everything you remembered would be different because you now remembered together, or decided to forget lest it hurt. I think every woman wants to make her husband a gift of certain memories, so that he can throw them away for her.

But it doesn't work that way with men like Gerald. They invite you into their lives, as a kind of staying guest. I've been doing quite well alone, thank you, but do come along for the ride. There's room for two. Mind now, don't bump into anything."

Her tone had sharpened, and she checked herself, putting her fish-knife to the fillet of sole and the tinned peas, with their bright false sheen.

"I sleep with Gerald," she gave the phrase a flat stress, "but there must be half a dozen men who know him better than I do, or ever shall. Who knew him at Brackens, or up at Magdalen, or in the war. The ones you drink with at the club. You've seen him cry when he was beaten and laugh when he won. You've heard him say the things men say when they are afraid and trying not to lie. You'd know what's wrong with him, what's cutting him to ribbons inside. He wouldn't have to tell you, because you wouldn't need to ask. It's the words and things you have between you, which you won't share. Not with me. Not with any woman."

She jerked out of control.

"Why don't you marry your college scouts, or the porter at the club? They'd know better than I how brown you want your toast, how to mend your cuffs and keep the place tidy. And they wouldn't nag you at night!"

He heard the crack in her voice, but before he could see the shimmer of tears, Sheila was on her feet and had brushed past him.

She came back after a few moments and drank her sauterne.

"I'm not going to apologize," she said it smiling and both laughed. For a spell, they chatted intently of odds and ends, of Reeve's authors and the latest Rosselini film. Then she looked down and tinged.

"Duncan, please try and answer what I'm going to ask. You know Gerald better than anyone. So much better than I do. You were always together. Try to remember. Has he ever had a child? Has he ever made another woman. . .?"

She stopped, her mouth thin, and her eyes on the plate.

"I have no idea, Sheila. I'm sorry, but I haven't a clue."

153

Even as he lied, the lie having come more swiftly, more easily than the will to deceive, Reeve felt a wave of affection break through him, of tenderness for the flat-boned young woman sitting across the table, now staring at her empty wine glass. With the lie came a strange, happy remorse. He wanted to lean over and touch her, to pass his hand along her cheeks and the shallow dip of her throat. He was dizzy with gentleness.

"Why did you ask, Sheila?"

"I'm not sure I know myself."

The fight had drained out of her. She pecked idly at the food.

"I thought it might be important. That it would help me understand where things have gone wrong."

"Does Gerald want children?"

"I do. I always have. Somehow I can't imagine being without them. Later on. And Gerald says he does. But so far. . . ."

She paused, off balance: "I'm not as modern as I pretend to be. I mean there are things I find it difficult to talk about. Even to someone as close to Gerald as you are."

Reeve touched her hand lightly: "Quite. I'm not very modern that way either. Vivianne used to laugh at me and say I was a prude. There are things I don't know how to listen to."

She took the plunge, with a faint, nervous twist of her shoulders: "I won't go into details. I wouldn't know how. But things haven't always been very good. Along *that* line. You know what I mean. Of late, they've been pretty awful."

She dabbed a finger across her dry lips, and again Reeve felt a surge of solicitude. It made him warm and inventive. He wanted to touch the bruise in her: "You don't need to tell me, Sheila, I've gone through hell that way." And with the astute shyness of a man talking sex to a woman he pities, Reeve began telling of Vi and himself, of the raw and sudden void between them, of how she had flung from the room one night in a dance of rage, her naked feet barely touching the ground.

But Sheila wasn't listening. Her own need was too blunt.

"I've said to Gerald, why don't we adopt a child? Maybe

154

it's an old-wives' tale, but they do say after you've adopted you often find you can have your own."

"And Gerald?"

"At first he didn't pay much attention. But when I pressed him, he went into a black mood. He said if anything was wrong, I was the one to blame. He could prove it. It wasn't any of my concern, but there had been something at Oxford which made him certain. Nothing like this had ever happened to him before." She was darkly flushed, but drove ahead, the cry for help loud inside her. "We had a frightful row. As if he was trying to slam a door between us. He hit me. It was the first time. Then he cried like a little boy. When he calmed down, he wanted me to . . ." She broke off with a shiver of distaste: "No, there's really nothing else to tell. When he said Oxford, I thought you might know. I'm sorry. Now I've gone and spilled it all over you. Perhaps I shouldn't have. I hate little girl talk. And I don't suppose these things are as rare or as awful as they seem at the time. But it helps to have someone listen." Her voice had the sour ring of tears.

Reeve pounced: "Tell me, Sheila, did that row take place just before the annual dinner?"

She nodded.

"Ah, that's it. That's why he made such a morbid ass of himself."

"So I gathered. But I've never managed to take your little table-rappings very seriously. Maybe you can explain. Why do perfectly reasonable, grown men, who publish books or assess real estate during the day, scurry off to play charades in the evening and get fearfully soused doing it?"

"Come off it, Sheila, you don't need me to tell you. All the chaps in there are hiding from their wives. Night off. There's candlery in heaven, all the husbands are put out!"

She didn't laugh: "I dare say."

Reeve parried: "You know it isn't that simple. You remember when you said a woman wanted to give her husband a parcel of memories, so he could tear them up for her and throw them away unopened, well, with men it's different. We need to take our memories out from time to time, and make sure there are no moths in them, that they haven't gone rotten on us. We like to know that they're as real and gilt-edge as we thought them. Take them away, tell us they've depreciated, that there's no market for them, and we're left bare."

Sheila focused: "Ah, that does help. I'm glad you've told me. Those things I don't know about and can't share with him. They're probably in a kind of safe, inside Gerald."

"Quite. And he has to take them out now and again. To give them an airing."

"Once a week," said Sheila.

Reeve looked up, puzzled.

"Why yes, or didn't you know? With A.G. up in Hampstead."

"A.G.?"

"Dr. Arthur Goldman. Gerald's being psychoanalysed. Weekly sessions. We'll soon be selling the furniture to pay for them. Surely you must have known. He tells you everything."

Reeve's ignorance and startled mien were an obscure triumph. She savoured it briefly and wondered.

"When did he start?"

"Just about the time you came back from America. The old dreams were coming on, so he couldn't sleep properly. The doctor wouldn't let him have any more pills and suggested he should see Goldman. Just to have a chat, you know. I suppose that's how they begin. I couldn't imagine that Gerald hadn't told you. Is that why you look so angry?"

Reeve drew a long breath: "I'm not angry. Why should I be? Gerald's a big boy now. He's got to decide for himself. And if he thinks it'll help. . . ."

"Don't you?"

"That's a pretty large subject, Sheila." He tried to say it lightly, but she saw him tense. "I wish I could go into it now" (he glanced busily at his watch) "but I can't. Back to the mines, I'm afraid."

They had coffee and said little, parting into their own thoughts. At the door of the restaurant, Reeve pulled himself erect.

"I'm awfully glad you've told me. You and Gerald mean the world to me. You know that, Sheila, don't you. There's really no one else I feel as close to. I'll do all I can to help, if I can. Let's see each other again soon. And keep the old chin up."

They shook hands warmly, as strangers do.

But instead of turning towards Great Russell Street, Reeve found himself hurrying west, his thoughts turbulent. He loathed psychoanalysis. The very word stung him to a cold passion. It had been the first shadow to fall between him and Vivianne. It was intimately a part of her world and speech. She moved in a circle in America where nearly everyone was in the game, where they gossiped of their analysis in a cunning chatter, of its blocs and transfers, of the analyst's sour breath or twitches. The first time he heard it, at a party in San Francisco, Reeve had understood: they were masturbating in public. And he had shouted it at them. Vi had turned, and warbled at him across her cigarette-holder: "Why, of course, you sweet dodo. Don't you think we know? But isn't that what you did in the little boys' room at Eton? And isn't it better than doing it alone?" They had laughed at him and told him to go read Reich on orgasm.

Reeve wasn't sure about God. On balance, he thought, probably not. But he could see that a man, in agony of spirit, might pour out to a priest the bile and refuse of himself. The priest being there as a mere cipher of the other presence, as a promise of God's ear. But to strip oneself naked before some Jewish twirp with cigarette stains on his cuff, to give him money every week so that one could empty into his lap one's garbage, the private parts, the privy in each of us—it made Reeve want to vomit. To pretend the old goat wasn't excited, that his own sex didn't rise when you told him of your itches and wet dreams! The whole thing was a dirty farce.

Reeve had known men tortured and starved hollow by the Germans, men who had their finger-nails torn out, one a day, and their balls smashed. And they hadn't broken. They'd held. Because being a human being was something fantastically strong, something it had taken unimaginable luck and decency to achieve. He had known women who came home to Stepney at the end of the night shift to find their home burnt off the face of the earth and their children ash. And after they'd screamed, they'd kept proud, and not asked anyone else to carry their pack of misery. But the one that uncoiled on the couches, or sat in the warm mud-bath of group therapy, what had they done, what had they endured, what Belsen, what desert? Bitches. Real bitches. Little girls in toreador pants and cashmere. Doing a weekly striptease. And paying a man to watch them. Reeve knew there were blokes who wanted to take off their trousers in public parks, and wave the thing at passers-by. Obscurely, he could feel the force of the impulse. But he found it resistible. Otherwise, what was the use of trying to be a human being? Why not give up, and become a dog pissing and fornicating in the sun?

Reeve tore along William IV Street. He knew, with jarring conviction, that he wasn't being truthful. Not all the way. It was more than his revulsion at analysis, more than a whiplash of abstract disgust. It had grown like a razor-edged cactus between him and Vi. Now it was taking Gerald away. Who was that quack in Hampstead? Who was he to barge in where Reeve had been the only, and the closest? What were his fingers prying for in the secret places which Reeve had shared, and of which he bore the key? He felt a tug of nausea, as if he had come home tired, and discovered the sheets in his bed faintly soiled. Why had Gerald not told him? Was Goldman's authority that great, that intimate already?

Reeve checked his stride and looked up. He found himself on

the steps of St. Martin-in-the-Fields, in a cry of pigeons. The truth came over him, blinding—he had had one divorce, he could not endure a second.

6

After that, Reeve lay in ambush. He had not long to wait. Gerald's requiem for the living dead had offended. The Desert Fathers met as before, but Brownlee wore an air of fastidious malaise, and some went home early. Pritchard could hardly conceal from himself that he found the singing less buoyant.

Two months after his lunch with Sheila Maune, Reeve had a call from Gerald: "We haven't had a real talk in a hell of a long time. There's something I want to ask you. Why don't we have a drink at the club before the dinner starts next Tuesday. Say we make it half past six."

Posted by the high window in the smoking-room, Reeve saw Gerald turn the corner of Londsdale Terrace. For a brief instant, he had the hallucination that he was looking at the wrong man. Maune had gotten paunchy, and in the sharp gust which swept the street his gait was imprecise. Reeve tautened his muscles, and noted with content that he himself had kept lean, that he would still be able, without shortness of wind, to follow the beagles over hedgerow and muddy ground, as he had done at Magdalen fifteen years before. But it was Maune's face— Reeve peered at it with the closeness of imperfect recognition— that arrested. It was a young face gone indecently old, without the buttress of intervening years. The hair was still flaxen at the temple and the chin unsteady; but the eyes were set deep and tired, and the skin was finely cracked. Like a new house, hurriedly plastered, and already flaking to dust.

They ordered drinks (the barman knew that Gerald took a double with only a wisp of tonic) and arched their legs against the fire-guard. Their talk strayed here and there, of taxes, of an acquaintance gone to New Zealand, of a libel action to which Reeve's firm was party. The old, easy cadence seemed between them.

Gerald went to fetch a second round. Bending over the back of Reeve's chair, the glasses poised in his hand, he asked with a casual drag in his voice: "I say, old man, you wouldn't happen to remember Ina? That girl I got involved with at Oxford?"

Reeve blinked at the fire and half turned his supple neck: "Ina? I'm not sure I do."

Gerald stirred heavily: "But you must. Don't you remember the funk I got myself into? I sat in your room and sweated like a frightened hog. Then you went and saw her."

"I do have a vague memory of the thing, now that you mention it. But she didn't make the same impression on me, old boy, as she obviously had on you."

Gerald coloured: "No. Of course she wouldn't. I was just wondering . . ." He faltered.

Reeve spun out the bogus silence: "You were wondering about what?"

"At the time I must have been too damn scared to ask. About what happened. Now I'd like to know. Whether she got herself taken care of," he winced saying it, "or whether she was going to have the baby."

"How should I know? I wouldn't have the foggiest notion."

"But surely you must. You went and talked to her. Don't you remember? She was to meet me in front of the Lamb and Flag. You were going to tell her what to do. She must have said something." The words had a dry, fuzzy taste in his mouth, like a blotter.

"I imagine I gave the little tart five quid and told her I'd call the police if she ever showed her face around Oxford again. But maybe it was only three. Yes, that's it. I gave her three pounds and she went off snivelling."

Gerald hunched forward, uneasy in his weight: "Look here, Flash," (it was a nickname Reeve hadn't heard since he ran for his house at Brackens, and it set his teeth on edge like a hint of blackmail) "I'm sure you know whether or not she was lying. I mean she *was* pregnant, wasn't she? And so there might have been a child."

Reeve leaned back in the dun mantle of his chair and spread his palms wide. He was amused to note how near to his mood were the stale postures of Victorian villainy: "How would I know?" He made reasonableness knife-sharp: "You *are* a nit! I'd almost forgotten the whole ballsup until you reminded me just now. How the devil should I know?"

"Because you weren't going to give her a farthing if she was lying. She wouldn't have stood a dog's chance with you, Flash. You liked things neat. And you were a great one for finding out."

Reeve mimed amazement: "Are you blaming me now? No, don't shake your head that way. I'm asking. Did I set asunder whom God had joined? You were going to kiss my hand when I came back to tell you it was all right. You were going to get down on your bloody knees, lad, and kiss my hand. Or don't you remember?"

"Come off it. You know damn well how grateful I was. And still am. It's just that I wanted to know about the baby."

"Why? What's all this about?"

Gerald made an odd gesture, as of a broken wing: "There are some things I've been trying to straighten out in my own mind. And I want to know. Very much."

A shard of live coal had tumbled from the grate; Reeve darted at it with his shoe.

"The whole thing's a blur. I don't even remember what the tart looked like. I've never given it another thought. But if it's any comfort to you, and you're making your peace with the Lord, thanks to St. Jude for favours received and all that, well I'll tell you, boy, she wasn't any more pregnant than my aunt

Sally! So stand easy. No one's going to turn up at the funeral and shout 'daddy'. You *are* a queer one."

Reeve came out of his chair making a face like a gargoyle, his long fingers to his chin and his face convulsed into an air of impish lechery. It was one of his best turns. But Gerald didn't laugh.

"You're sure of that?"

"Absolutely. She played you for a patsy. She saw what a soft touch you were and tried to pull a fast one. Pregnant? Don't make me laugh." He exhaled with mock finality.

"You're lying," said Gerald, "I don't know how I can be so sure," (the knowledge had sprung upon him, with a jarring, sickening impact), "but I know it. You're lying."

And in the moment he said it, all changed. The contour of the room, the bite of smoke and cold in the air, the yellow of the lamp, the rub of the tweed suit against his wrist. All changed utterly. A huge, dim shape had passed across the light making the heart hammer and be still.

He said it once more: "You're lying to me." Not in hatred, but in amazement before the breadth and simplicity of his ruin. The shrill of the lie had sounded out of the depths of Reeve, and Gerald had heard it resonant in the room, derisive. There need never be a second. The scratch was unalterable in the voice. To hear a lie in a friend, and Reeve had been the sharer and strong shadow of him, was to hear the soft start of death. It changes all.

Reeve did not know whether he was lying; perhaps the falsehood lay only in the easy stress he had put on his denial. But Maune's outrage, and what he dimly perceived of withdrawal and contempt, goaded him like the sight of an open wound. He would not let silence pass judgment: "Look here, old boy, I've had a hard day. I don't know what you're after, or why you should think I'm lying. I've never been in such a bloody silly argument in my whole life. Okay. Have it your way. She was going to have twins. I could hear them saying 'where's poppa?

162

Where's old man Maune?' We decided to name them Jeremy and Egbert and put them down for Eton. Now be a good chap and get me a drink, will you. Christ. You'd think *I'd* knocked her up."

"Forget it. I don't care to talk about it any more."

Gerald stood quite near, but Reeve had difficulty hearing him, as if a sudden turbulence had cut between. A sour spasm gripped him, and his skin went hot: "I don't know what the hell's biting you. But don't take it out on me. I'm telling you, boy. Don't you take it out on me!"

"Keep your shirt on, old man. I'm not saying anything."

"I'm fed up sitting here and having you look at me as if I'd stolen money off a blind man. Who the hell are you calling a liar? It's time you grew up, Maune. I'm telling you for your own good."

"Why are you getting so excited? I said, forget it."

He spoke it kindly, there being room for kindness and tact in the new emptiness. Reeve heard the note. It made his nerves leap, and he lunged out like a runner stumbling: "Are you patronizing me? Well, *are* you?"

Gerald looked away, and made a vague motion towards the bar.

But Reeve pulled him close: "Look Maune, *I'm* not your analyst."

Being in a new world, where touch and voice betrayed, Gerald was not startled.

"Ah. So you know. Of course. Sheila must have told you. She's cut up about it. She thinks it'll ruin us. Probably true."

"That's not the reason, and you know it. She can't bear the thought of you making an ass of yourself. Of your doing something so utterly bogus."

Reeve felt back in the saddle. He poured out his derision of psychoanalysis, his intimate, contemptuous knowledge of the havoc it created among his American acquaintances. His arguments flashed bright and crowded as from a Roman candle: "You're having a rough patch with Sheila. All right, I don't want to know the details. None of my business. Nor anybody else's. I don't suppose there's a marriage going that doesn't have its bad stretches. Right from the start, and when I was most involved, there were days when I looked at Vi and had grit in my mouth. Fair enough. That's the old snake's apple in our throats. Thou shalt sow thy seed in stony furrows and sweat thy balls off doing it. But you're a big boy now. You're the only one who can make a go of it. You and Sheila. And you know damn well there's nothing I wouldn't do to help, if you want me to. So why open your fly and wave the bloody thing at some Hebe in Hampstead, and pay the old goat for leering?"

Gerald listened, but found it hard to place the man who was addressing him with such insistent flourish. The voice was familiar, but somehow off pitch, as if it had passed through a fret of static.

"You've got to stand on your feet, lad. To stop leaning. There was always someone, wasn't there? At home, it was mum. And crikey, she was a strong one. At school, it was me. You remember the day you passed out in the yard? You held on to me as if I were the Lamb of God. I don't know who it was in Cairo, but you looked as if you had a pair of golden crutches. Someone was carrying you. Right on top of the bloody wave. Well it's time you got out of the old womb."

"I suppose it's true. I've never been as clever as you, or as sure of myself. Perhaps I always *have* needed someone to prop me up. I won't deny it. But if you think that's what Goldman does, you couldn't be more wrong. When I'm with him, I have to walk alone. Farther than I ever wanted to or thought my legs could carry me. You remember that obstacle course they made us slog through, with the bloody sergeant-major bellowing and waving a stick at you. There was a mound of earth you had to run up and jump from, into a lot of muck and water.

164

They made us do it at night. I'll never forget that. I was so scared I nearly wet myself. Falling into a black hole, and the air hitting you. Well, it's hard to explain. But it's rather like that. He kicks you off the edge, and you come down all shivery and not wanting to move. But you pick yourself up and start crawling in the dark. Somehow. And I'd never have believed you could be so alone with someone else sitting right behind you in the same room."

His face lit with an expression of wry love.

"You look like a bobby-soxer swooning," taunted Reeve.

Gerald smiled, out of reach: "It's terribly difficult trying to explain to anyone who hasn't gone through it. Who's outside. There are times when I feel it's the realest thing that's ever happened to me, and the only thing that will help. Other days, I loathe the whole business and want to chuck it. Once, I remember wanting to take Goldman by the neck and strangle the voice out of him. It was like a dentist's drill."

Again he smiled, in a recollection so rich and private that it jarred on Reeve like a door closed against him.

"But don't you see the whole thing's a fraud, an utter fraud? That he's just a quack sniffing at a lot of garbage? Jesus, boy, you don't have to have a Nanny any more to wipe your bottom when you've been to the toilet. That's all he's doing. Don't you understand?"

"I've always thought you were the cleverest chap I knew. I never dared argue with you. But right now you sound stupid. My fault. I'm sorry I ever bothered you with all this. Let's just forget it. Anyhow, time to go."

He said it easily, looking up at the clock, but it had an undercurrent, drawing the present occasion towards a dim, cold finality.

"I'm warning you. If you don't stop seeing that charlatan, and making a show of yourself like you did here the other night, you'll lose Sheila. And you're not a one to go alone. I'm telling you, Maune, not alone!"

"Sorry, old man, but as you say, I've been leaning too much. I've got to decide this one for myself."

"You've got to listen to me. I can prove the thing's a bloody racket. That you're being taken for a ride. I can *prove* it!"

Beneath the angry mask of Reeve's face and his darting finger, Gerald heard the wail of jealousy. It threw him off balance.

"I wonder what Goldman would say hearing you. Why does it matter to you so dreadfully? Why do you hate it so? You should look at yourself in the mirror. You're all white. Perhaps I'm not the one who needs it most."

"Meaning what?"

Gerald sought to break clear, but it was too late. Their intimacy had gone overripe. Now it burst, and a rancid venom spilled.

"Meaning that you haven't done so well either, Flash." The nickname mocked. "I was only saying to Sheila the other day: Duncan hasn't gotten over it, has he? Walks around like a ghost. Don't we know anyone we could introduce him to? A nice girl with a bit of money and a garden."

Being full of their new hatred, and savouring its cool, bracing fumes, they both calmed down. Drink left Reeve's intelligence armed and ungoverned.

"Look here, Maune, make you a bet. Give me three weeks and I'll prove to you that Dr. Goldman's a fraud. That the whole thing is utterly bogus."

Gerald listened, as to a bright, dangerous child.

"He asks you about your dreams, doesn't he?"

"Yes, that's the most important thing. It starts you off. Pushes you off the jump."

"And the dream is supposed to take the old letch right inside you, down to the balls of your soul."

"I wouldn't put it that way."

"But that's the whole point, isn't it?"

"I suppose so. It opens the door. Like going down a staircase inside yourself."

166

"And no one else's dreams would do? I mean dreams people told you, or you'd read in a book?"

"Of course not. What a stupid idea. Like showing an X-ray of your aunt Tilly when you wanted to find out about your own lungs."

"Exactly. And if a doctor couldn't tell which was which you'd know him for a ponce, wouldn't you?"

"Look, old man, time's a'passing. Hadn't we better go in now?"

But Reeve pulled him down, his knuckles aching.

"I told you I can prove it. How often do you go there? Twice a week, is it? All right. Give me three weeks. I'll make up some dreams for you. A whole packet of them. And you'll learn them by heart. They'll be short enough, I can tell you. And you'll spew them out for old Siegmund Fraud exactly as if they were your own, as if *you*'d dreamt them. And he won't catch on. He'll put his nose to them just as if they *were* your own. And you'll crawl down the shaft together. But it won't be you. It won't be you at all!"

"That's absurd! You *are* a silly ass. Why should I waste my time lying to him?"

"Because you'd see with your own eyes that the thing stinks. That it's as fake as card-tricks. Because you'd realize that he's making a sucker of you. That you're getting the finger right up you, boy, right where the old Yid can smell the money."

Reeve pitched back in his chair, quivering and hoarse with delight.

"You make me sick," said Gerald, but he said it with a dull uncertainty.

Reeve crowded in, the lash of the harpoon whistling in his tone: "Three weeks. I'm not asking for much. Maybe he'll see through it. But you don't really believe that, do you, Maune? You're afraid. You're all shaking inside, aren't you?"

"Leave off, will you. Just leave off."

"One hundred pounds. I'm betting you one hundred pounds.

And I'm in your hands. One wink, one giggle and he'll smell a rat. But I trust you. You're going to repeat those dreams just as if you'd dreamt them the night before, as if they'd made you wet the bed. I trust you like I wouldn't trust anyone else in the world." He said it with acid relish. "One hundred pounds to back up your new god. It's cheap, boy, it's cheap."

Gerald was on his feet. He felt that if he struck out with his fist, accurately, the crazy wasp of a voice would stop whirring. Gin had made him heavy, but he sensed that he must rivet his attention, that the instant was like a top spinning, and could fall into an evil shambles. Still the wasp sang and stung.

"One hundred pounds." He said it to himself. And saw, at the same moment, that they were not alone.

Brian Smith had come over from the bar, all ears: "I say, are you chaps making a bet?"

"We are," said Reeve.

"What about?"

"That I can dream his own dreams for him, and no one the wiser."

"You're a fool, Reeve. Why should I do it?" He said it without conviction. The thing was dragging him down, away from the light. He had crossed the imperceptible shadow-line, leaving behind the feel of his own will.

"I'll be dashed if I understand a word you're saying. But one hundred pounds! I say." And Smith glowed with excitement. He turned to the barman: "Timms, will you hand me the betting-book. There's a good chap."

He opened the clasp and turned the yellowed pages, the high note and rebuke of ancient wagers faded to a wraith-like scrawl. "Anyone know the date?"

Timms read off the calendar.

"Righti-o. D. Reeve bets Gerald Maune that he can . . ." He faltered, perplexed. ". . . I say, how did you put it? . . . dream his dreams for him and no one the wiser. For the sum of £100."

Smith stared at what he had written, but a beautiful stupidity carried him before the wind. Gerald signed as if it was a tortuous joke, having nothing to do with him. Nothing real. He would wake from it as from the hammering dullness in his brain.

"Witness: Brian Smith. I'll be dashed. A hundred quid. Crikey." He hurried out brimful.

Through the open door, Gerald saw the Desert Fathers gathered and waiting. He drove his hand through his dampened hair and turned to go. But Reeve caught him smartly by the elbow.

"I'll send you the first tomorrow."

"The first what?"

"Why your first dream, old boy, your first dream."

And as he followed Gerald, Reeve's body seemed, for an instant, in the grip of a wild, secret dance.

7

"*Gerald Maune.* G.M. George Medal. Grand Marnier. G. M. Trevelyan. If I had got that Trinity Fellowship. All the difference. Walnuts and port in the Combination Room the first night you're made a Fellow. Read about it in Hardy. *Jus primae noctis.* The Jews of the first night. Trevelyan striding up and down that long room on the afternoon war broke out. Crying. Why don't you say it? Why don't you tell me that I've been an utter fool about Mr. Hitler. *Mr.* Hitler. The Fellows silent. Listening to their own bowels. Old frauds. But I wanted it. God how I wanted it. Lukes got it. Tall pimply sadist. Voice like a cracked flute. But Eton. And fathers and grandfathers prebendaries of where was it? Chichester. Or St. Asaph. Best thing I ever wrote. *Hume on Causation in the Light of the New Psychology.* Craven meeting me in Great Court. Decent buzzard. Voted for you, Goldman. But no good. Sorry. Bit of advice, old chap. Bad thing in England to be clever; unforgivable to show it. Lights in the Combination Room that night. Knew Lukes was in there. Went to my room and masturbated into the wash-basin. Hadn't done *that* for a long time. All the difference. Wouldn't be here in Hampstead. Four patients a day. Not bad actually. But oh the *meschugene* crap. Nearly always the same. More or less. And Irving coming up to my room the next morning, seeing the closed trunk. Cheer up, *mensch*. Did you really think they'd elect you to the College of Heralds?"

From the labyrinth of his resentment, still acid, came sudden laughter.

"I might not have met Hannah. First time we did it, on the floor, by the electric fire in her bed-sitter off Belsize Park. Does she still have those slacks? Green velvet. Probably not. Big in the hips now. But that time on the floor. Like the trumpets of Jericho. And the landlady sniffing at us as we went out. Now Aaron. I love him. Yea more than the apple of mine eye. Queer expression. *Augenapfel*. But I don't like him much. Soft, and where he hardens, a kind of cunning. Not like Hannah or me at all. Moves like uncle Reuben. Same trick of the shoulder. But Judith. Does one really want to fornicate with one's daughter? And if she fell for a *goy*? Indiscretion. A stranger reading the family letters. Because that's where the memories are. In the black box. The old memories between the legs. Childe Roland to the dark tower came. Browning knew. Poets always know. No one to listen. We live off dead poets. Friend Oedipus. Good title. Must tell Rudi. Tennyson at Trinity the night of the feast. All the Fellows lined up, white tie and scarlet. The candle-sheen on the dark wood. How I wanted it. Each stepping forward to meet the Great Man. Oscar Browning, small and fat. I'm Browning. Tennyson, after long silence. No, Sir, you're not."

This time, Dr. Goldman laughed loud, and pulled out a corner of his handkerchief to wipe his misted spectacles. *Gerald Maune*. The dossier was on the blotter, thick and untidy at the edge. He stooped his back to harness.

"Where did I lose control? When did it go wrong? Too easy at the start. When McIvers sent him to me. Decent of McIvers. Doesn't really believe in analysis. Scrapped like dogs when we were both at the Maudsley. Doesn't like Jews either. In that special British way. Thinks history has given us such a raw time, that we've all got bad breath. *Suspected jaundice. Symptoms of hepatitis or possible anaemia. Biopsy negative.* Re-examination after three months. Complaints of insomnia and compulsive dreaming. Loss of appetite but steady increase of weight. Consumption of alcohol probably greater than patient admits or is fully aware of. Obvious even to McIvers where the roots lie. Charcot to Freud: *les vraies causes sont dans l'alcôve.* One of the great moments of history. No bells. And for S.F. no Nobel. Why does the brain pun more when it's tired?

"Came to me April 11th. Two years ago. Nightmares. Of men burning and their voices turning to birds. Birds, *vögeln* = to fuck. The birds diving down with their beaks, tearing. In the beginning was the pun. After the dreams, nights when he couldn't. Complete fiasco. Mrs. M. trying to help. Probably more intelligent than he. Sudden erections during the day. Embarrassing. These things had never happened before. Lying, of course. They all lie during the first months. Lying on the couch. The lie of the lay. The lay of the lie. *Lorelei.* Ballad of our craft. Clear that it had never really been satisfactory between them. *Coitus interruptus* at the start. Then the decision to have children. Premature ejaculation. When at all. Blames her. Savage on this.

"June 19th. First time I felt ground. Strange feeling that. Like coming out of muddy water. Meaningless. Then, all of a sudden, solid ground. Something in the voice, or a twist of speech. A real word under the cliché. The darkness visible. We and the poets. Blind to hear better."

Dr. Goldman brushed cigarette ash from a page of notes. He wrote on foolscap in a small, crowded hand.

"June 19th. The first dream that spoke loud. A woman un-
doubtedly his wife. But in profile. And legs like a man. M.
trying to reach her. Digging. Wet sand sliding across his
hands. She is not buried in the sand, but on top or to one
side of it. Nevertheless, fierce compulsion to dig. She turns
the other way. M. calls as loud as he can, but is not certain
she can hear. Wakes, with the name Cold Harbour distinct
in his conscious memory."

They had quarrelled two days before. Leaving a dinner party,
Mrs. M. had said that he drank too much. No one else at the
table had taken three glasses of port. *Port* and *harbour*. M.
recalled at once that it was a bottle of Sandeman's port. *Sand-
man,* the bringer of sleep, or the place of thirst, of dunes that
shift and choke. *Cold* because, as he had remarked to Mrs. M.,
the J's never served any of their wines at a proper temper-
ature.

So far, only surface. M. himself makes the verbal connections.
"Like a double-acrostic." We talk of Torquemada, the pen-
name of the contriver of the most difficult acrostics. M. has
read somewhere that Torquemada is, in real life, a school-
master. "A man who can dream up those fiendish things every
week must be a terror with the old cane."

June 25th:
    M. is in a large hall with mullion windows. He is to one
side, but when he cranes his neck, he can make out a high
gallery, and in the shadows, men watching. In the hall, there
are clothes-racks, most of them bare. Someone—*this part of
the dream is unclear*—is saying that he has come too late. Most
of the clothes are sold. He sees another rack hung with belts
and braces. Starts choosing. The person selling them is Mrs.
M. Whatever item he picks, she drops awkwardly to the
floor. M. is very angry: "This is a job for someone older.
You're too young to do it properly." The personage—he is
no longer quite sure it is Mrs. M.—starts laughing. The

figures in the gallery laugh also. The echoes reverberate, and M. is suddenly in a swimming bath. He is wearing gloves.

A number of strands are obvious. Torquemada, head of the Inquisition: hence the word *rack* (clothes-rack). Fear or desire of nakedness (M. is himself aware of the implications of *"You've come too late. Most of the clothes are sold"*). The hall suggests the school refectory, and the swimming bath, with its splashing echoes, is the one at Brackens. M. recalls that the boys swam naked, and how uncomfortable that made him at the start.

Why the gloves? M. apparently does not know that *mullein* (*mullion* windows) is the common name of a species of flowers known in America as fox-*glove*. Tries to evade my insistence on the point. Finally provides his own explanation. M. often passes through a street behind Charing Cross on his way to work. Store with surgical appliances, rubber goods, trusses, and usual books on sex-hygiene and perversion. Two have caught his eye: *A History of Flogging* (cover shows a man stripped to the waist, *braces* hanging loose, being flogged against a kind of wooden cross-bar), and *Records of the Holy Inquisition* (a monk bending over a blurred, female figure, nude and tied to a *rack*). Just underneath the books, a display of rubber gloves, one of them on a stand, erect, long-fingered. M. is disturbed and excited at the idea of such gloves being used *ad anum*. He realized that the dream signifies far more than appears, that these surface recognitions are only the outworks. But he refuses to look deeper.

August 3rd. A month lost. Two appointments not kept. One cut to twenty minutes: "sorry, I have had no dreams this week. I must be getting well." M. obstructing, and conscious that he is doing so. Today the dam broke.

He asked me to draw the shades: "I have a touch of migraine." Could he see the notes I had taken on *that* dream? I read him his own version of it without comment. "I suppose there's something you should know, if you don't already." M. explains that the failure of *coitus* is due to his wife's passiveness, to the time it takes to get her stimulated ("it's like digging through sand"). She expects foreplay but gives nothing in return. M. has often hinted that he would like "to try something new", to explore. But she is indifferent or queasy.

He came home from the pub one night ("I won't deny I was a bit liquored up"). Always hangs his belt or braces across a chair near the bed when undressing. *Ejaculatio praecox*. M. annoyed and embarrassed. Determined to provoke second erection. Hands Mrs. M. his belt and lies on the bed face-down. She gives him a light tap. Then starts laughing (same sound as in the dream). She can't do it. If he needs "that kind of thing", he'll have to find it elsewhere. Later that night, the dream and involuntary pollution.

M. is bitter and talkative: "I know it's a queer thing to ask. But I was drunk, and there are things they want us to do to them. Pretty nauseating, if you ask me. But part of the game, I suppose." He voices the conviction that English women are notoriously passive, that they want sex "served up like tea, with a dash of sugar and cream, and thank you, James, you may go now". Ask them for a touch of invention, for "something a bit special", and they look at you "as if you'd been caught buggering the vicar's goldfish". Lewd as cats in their own way, but not letting on. "Make you feel like a slave or a ruddy sexmaniac." He had met a girl in France: "She went all white when she touched me. And used the words for the things she wanted us to do. Sheila wouldn't be caught dead saying those words. She doesn't say anything. Like making love to a mute."

M. claims to know a lot of men who feel as he does: "You'd be surprised whom you'll find in Soho on a weekday afternoon. Businessmen, dons, chaps from the bank. Going into the little doorways on Frith Street. French model, second floor. *Correction. Special massage.* I don't fancy that kind of place myself. But I can see where a perfectly decent chap might be driven to it. We had it better, over there, in the war. I suppose that's the root of it."

Pours out stories of what he had come in the way of, or heard about, in Egypt, Naples, France: "Bloke in my battalion had two sisters doing it to him in a house just outside Naples. Kept them naked, right from breakfast on. Girls who meant it. Not just doing you a bloody favour. Or setting their jaws as if they were playing hockey for Roedean."

I let him talk and thrash about until he himself didn't believe it. Until he could hear himself lying.

Why the *gallery*?

M. looked at his watch and apologized for running beyond the hour. I told him it was important. He didn't have a clue. He offered to go and try and remember before the next time. I said we might be near the beginning of a coherent pattern, that if we didn't break through now the defence mechanisms would grow more tenacious, and the track more difficult to follow. Why the *gallery*?

Moment of truth. It always comes in analysis. Sometimes after six months or a year; sometimes when it is too late. The crack in the voice. Unmistakable. Half fear, half bravado. Even in the *Angst*, the unbreakable little core of vanity. The patient to himself: I *am* an interesting case. Otherwise the old bird wouldn't be listening so intently, he wouldn't be prying so hard.

"There was a gallery like that in the Upper School library. The library was where the prefects met, and you were called up for your beating. I wasn't caned often, mark you. I was rather mousey and kept low. But some nasty little rotter put ink in the shoe-polish, and when I did the house-captain's shoes, they came out a fearful mess. So I got six. And I can tell you Frank March had a powerful wrist. Played lacrosse for Sandhurst later on."

Did he remember anything else about the occasion?

"Yes, now that you mention it. I wet my bed that night. Not

in the way you might think. The *other* way. It was the first time. I was frightened out of my wits, but wanted it to happen again. Kept my eyes shut, waiting. Odd, isn't it? But they do say there's nothing like a beating to make a man of you."

Goldman leaned back, his vision bleary. Though he had come across exactly this same pattern, this rusted trap, in numerous cases, it still stirred him to a dull rage. The black idiocy of it. He often wondered what resilience or bluntness of nerve kept the general run of ex-public school men out of mental homes. In Soho, the rate was said to be one pound a stroke. Clearly an upper-class trade. Mrs. M. must have understood. She was too alert not to. But she had wanted no part of it. Goldman had never met Sheila Maune, but he knew that women could make of their poise and sufficiency a weapon against a man's need.

He recalled how that hour (it was, in fact, nearer two hours) had ended. After a complete silence, Gerald came off the couch like a switch-blade closing: "I know what's in your mind, Doctor. I know exactly. You think I'm a queer. That deep down I'm queer! That I'm a masochist or something. That's what you call it, isn't it? Well, isn't it?"

Goldman had expected him to shout. But not so loud.

"You think you're on to it, don't you? That you've got the living gut out of me. That I'm some kind of crazy queer who needs to be beaten! God almighty, you make me sick. You're no better than the others. You don't even want to understand."

He had controlled himself, but in a false way, like an actor poised for exit. He had taken the money out of his bill-fold and dropped it on Goldman's desk: "That *is* what I owe you, I believe."

Goldman caught a faint savour from somewhere in the house. It lit on his tongue. Pot roast, with heavy, dark gravy and garlic. Hannah must be in the kitchen. He stirred in his chair, his attention cast wide and downstream. Then he reeled in, hunching his mind. He pulled out the next page in the file and turned on the desk lamp.

There had been no word until September 1st. *Memorandum:* "Call from McIvers, himself rather shaken. On the night of the 24th.8., Mrs. M. had asked him to come. M. in excruciating pain. Unable to lie down or straighten fully. Insomnia and accelerated consumption of spirits during previous fortnight. *Examination for kidney-stones negative.* Provisional diagnosis: slipped disk and inflammation of the nervous tissue. Aetiology obviously psychosomatic. M. both depressed and obsessively anxious about the prospect of resuming analysis. McIvers calling on his behalf. I concurred immediately, and predicted that pain would subside rapidly.

"First appointment, September 5th. M. shows signs of physical fatigue, but is anxious to please, to 'play fair' and 'give it a real chance'."

The next weeks, however, had been unsatisfactory. Maune talked in a compulsive stream, but the associations and snatches of dream-imagery which he offered were logically contrived. He was striving to win Goldman's approval. During the process of transference, even patients of mediocre intelligence marshal an extraordinary cunning. They tender to the analyst, as a gift trimly ordered, the skein and clues he has privately unravelled. He must guard himself against the seduction of their hope. It was, Goldman recalled, a bizarre duel.

Now he leafed slowly through the notes and memoranda covering the subsequent months. On the corner of one page, he had doodled a rough graph of the case, with its characteristic curve—small rises followed by sharp drops, monotonous plateaux and moments of recoil or backlash when all the work accomplished seemed like blank waste.

You thrash away from the wreck, somehow, blindly. The suction pulls you under, into the drag of black water and black oil. Your lungs burst with the cold filth pouring in. Each time you flail to the surface, the downdrag gets stronger. So does the temptation to let go, to swallow the muck and have done. But the whirlpool vomits you to the light, and you find yourself swimming. There is someone swimming just to one side and a little behind you, and at first the shore looks near, say half a year off, like an unwavering line between the trough of the waves. But it comes no closer. When you crane your neck, with enormous effort, to see beyond the grey heave of water, the line has vanished or changed direction. You are kept going by the stroke of the swimmer behind you. It has the beat of sane purpose, it seems to know where you're going. But it doesn't hold you up, or very little. And you come to loathe the drive of it with a spent hatred. Sometimes, with immense luck, you reach shore. Usually, it's only a spit of brackish sand, with more seas on the other side. There is no certain end to an analysis, no warm and promised earth for the soul to drowse on unguarded. At best, you will learn to swim with the cold and treasons of the current, rather than against, and you will dive into the deep not for oblivion, but for its secret, nocturnal roots which, when we touch them with salutation and reserve, yield us what power we have to endure on the mutinous waves.

It was the antique allegory of the mind's harassed voyage. Goldman had learnt the force of it during his own training analysis. With each case, he felt its truth renewed.

Maune started out bravely. If this evil thing lurked inside him, he would come to know it full-face. But he could not believe that it *was* evil. On the contrary. The probe had touched a central nerve. Hence the gust of rage and the flight from the net. The intimacy with Reeve wove its skein around the core of his own life. Nothing in that life had been finer, richer of meaning, than the brief companionship of Jan K. in Cairo, in 1942. Now the strong place had been broken open and pillaged, the last of his possessions strewn in a hard light. Maune felt as if he had taken a hammer to his own skull.

In December, Goldman had set down a summary of the case,

a contour of work in progress. It was written in a code of brevity, of wilful simplification, and as he read it now, his lips miming, irony assailed him.

"Classical preconditions for sexual ambivalence: early death of father; the mother a dominant force; a house full of sisters. In school, the development of the libido was inevitably associated with latent homosexual patterns. M. is himself aware of the coincidence between corporal punishment and erotic stimulation. Coincidence looms large in his onanistic fantasies. In R. he found a substitute father-figure, one who judges, punishes and protects.

"The affair at Oxford, with its accidental pregnancy (?), confirmed the pattern of ambivalence. M. was apparently seduced by a woman who exhibited initiative and specific masculine traits (he recalls her *rough voice* and *broad hands*). By sending R. in his place, he subconsciously denied his own sexual responsibility. The fear and humiliation were traumatic. Yet, at the same time, M. buttressed his ego with the conviction that he had proved his virility, that he had performed the part of the man and the father.

"Then came the war, with its re-enactment of school fantasies and rituals. The pack mauling and yelling in the field, body to body, only more naked than rugger. The latent homosexual impulses hover near. In the amorous sweat of groundcrews waiting for their pilots to come home. The kilted boys play the pipes, and the officers stride into combat behind them, carrying their canes. Many of the women met were brown or olive. They did not speak proper English. Hence they were outside the rules. One could ask them or pay them to *do the things* middle-aged men and boys have fantasies about when they masturbate.

"For Maune, the war meant separation from R. But it brought the chuminess of the ward room and the affair with Jan K."

(At this point, Goldman had doodled a question mark, and

179

it had spiralled into a chaotic serpent. He began to skip inter vening pages.)

"M.'s motives for wanting a child are complex. Compulsive desire to prove to himself and his wife that he is *normal*, that he can have children like any other man. At the same time, he has an acute, neurotic insight into the fact that a child keeps a woman busy, that it compensates for a certain diminution of sexual activity. It takes off the pressure. The idea of adoption was intolerable precisely because it leaves open the question of personal sexual adequacy. In many English middle-class families, children are not necessarily a proof of sustained sexual interest; they may represent evasion from it, or compensation. Complicated subject; needs to be clarified.

"With R.'s return from America, M.'s dormant homosexuality, and the associated masochistic fantasies, were intensely activated. The neurosis declared itself (symptoms of jaundice, spells of insomnia, heavy drinking, the severe back pains in August). The rebellion against the super-ego, with its heterosexual demands and standards, assumed drastic forms. The danger of a manic-depressive cycle, or of complete nervous collapse, cannot be ruled out. M. himself seems aware of this, and the analysis is showing progress."

He pushed the file away, and a shrug passed through his stooped shoulders. A glass, or a knife clicking against a plate, sounded from somewhere in the house. G-minor, thought Goldman, the key of evening.

All very neat, like a case in the textbooks or the *Traumdeutung*. The Sphinx lay on her back purring. But what relation did it have to the vital disorder, to the singularity of a man's ruin? No more than had the mite of tissue, mounted on a slide, to the multitudinous weave and cunning of organic life.

Exasperation rose in him, like bile. What should he have done?

"I am not God, though there are moments in analysis when the analyst takes on a queer authority, when he pities or torments as God does His creatures. 'Give the patient's ego *freedom* to choose one way or the other.' The italics are the Master's. But that's arrogance and self-deception. How can he choose, how can we ask him to, in a society whose laws and expectations are outside our control? We do not live in a vacuum where all rational possibilities could, in fact, be explored. Suppose I had said to Maune: stop this bitter, suicidal process of repression. Let the energies and drives of the id penetrate your ego instead of undermining it. Your present mode of emotional and sexual life is a legal fiction, built on the needs others have felt for you, not on your own. This obsessive desire to conceive a child is a mask. If the homosexual compulsion asserts itself—and it is probably less frequent or exclusive than you unconsciously fear —don't choke it down at the price of your health and sanity. If you need to be slapped on the buttocks once in a while in order to live at peace with the energies of your psyche, with its receptive and creative powers, don't make a production of it. Go to it, as a man might do when he has to relieve himself against a hedge. The psyche can burn as sharply as the bladder. There is hardly a human being alive in our crazy warren who doesn't have a poisonous itch under the skin. You're luckier than most, because you've seen yours, not for a dragon, but for what it is—a cumbersome, ugly, but by no means rare house-pest. Don't pretend it isn't there. Live with it. Easier to let it have dog-biscuit than raven on your own flesh.

"But what right have I to say that if I can't, at the same time, reorganize our whole *meschugene* society? If I can't cry from the roof-tops that half the marriages I know about among men of that type and class are a sham? I'm neither God nor the Archbishop of Canterbury. What should I have done? And if our culture were to change, to change radically, who would need psychiatry?"

Goldman yielded to a familiar vertigo. Unawares, his hands sketched an immemorial gesture of ironic defeat, palms raised and outspread.

"I didn't even try to say those things. I did nothing to subvert M.'s belief that he could work "*this garbage*" out of his system. And the crust of illusion was beginning to harden and take life when those other dreams came."

Goldman sought to make hindsight scrupulous. He *had* known. Not exactly, but as in the hot doze of a fever, when we know that we are not ourselves, not only. Just out of reach, another presence loomed. It was in the room during those three weeks, and he had waited for it to spring. It crouched in Gerald's voice, in his meticulous, absorbed apartness, the man listening to himself, rigid and dizzy, like someone bending from a great height. Goldman *had* realized—he was not consoling himself now, after the fact—that Gerald's words were not directed at him, or only obliquely, that he was overhearing a dialogue, as of wrestlers careening in the room, their teeths clenched.

These dreams were compact and luminous, like a spray of poison-berries. With gashes of bright colour, where M.'s preceding reveries had been invariably dun.

Ash-trees calling, coughing in the wind, and when the dreamer lunged out of the house, naked, the branches shearing loose like birds, and burying him with reeking droppings. Dreams that showed a puerile, sadistic wit. M. in an empty house, the phone ringing. Water rising from the floor. M. compulsively anxious to find the receiver. Feels himself drowning. Woken, inside the dream, by a man saying: "I wanted to give you a toot on the blower." M. sees the man turning to the wall and hears a drilling sound. Wakes with the nursery-twister— peck of pickles—on his tongue. The *blower*, the *pecker*, the rise of water, all beautifully ravelled. The repressed fantasies of the libido seemed to have torn loose. They were stomping through the psyche in a crude devil's dance. Too crude. Goldman had sensed it. Same feeling if he had observed Maune entering the consulting room unwashed.

Alien splinters in Maune's usual speech. Like the Americanism in the nightmare turning on the ambiguity of *deck* (a *deck* of cards, the *deck* of a boat).

That lewd fragment: a beggar unscrewing his leg, urinating on a chess-board full of pawns, and saying to M. that he had to hurry back to his shop. When Goldman had drawn attention to the coil of meaning (beggar-peddlar-piddler-*pédale*, the common French slang for homosexual; the obvious castration gesture, and the connotations of *screw*; the old, randy joke about meeting at the *pawn-shop* to kiss under the balls), Gerald had shown no disgust, only an uncanny, tense fascination.

The suspicion that some game was being played, that Maune was compounding these strident dreams out of a manual of psychopathology, had crossed Goldman's mind. Gerald would not have been the first. At moments when the ego lay fallow or gagged, other patients had filched dreams out of novels and even the works of Freud, either to trick the analyst, or not to come empty-handed.

Why had he not challenged him straight out? Simply because these dreams had a gross but intimate relevance. They were a brutal mimicry of the covert, tentative shadowplay of repression and censorship, but they followed closely the contours of Maune's neurosis. In one of the notes he took during the second week, Goldman had scribbled the word *schizophrenia*? But he had crossed it out. It did not fit the case. Some part of M. appeared to have broken out of the grip of identity. Goldman recalled the strange passage in Aquinas which defines ghosts as shreds of our psyche, momentarily transmuted into pure force. Listening to those dreams, he had felt the dim feverishness of the ghost brushing his skin. But he had not wanted to arrest what might be a dangerous, yet ultimately healing trick of the subconscious.

That was why he had not responded to Maune's provocation: "is there nothing *you* want to say, Dr. Goldman, nothing you want to tell me?" Nor had been unduly perturbed when Gerald announced that he was off on a business trip for a couple of weeks, that he was planning "to use up the expense account".

Once more, Goldman raked over in his mind every detail of that Friday afternoon. He felt certain—or almost—that the shock of a secret need had passed through him. That he was on the point of calling Maune back from the door to ask—where are those dreams from? What vulgar devil is running your life just now? But, in fact, he had said no more than: "Very well, I'll be waiting to hear from you when you're back." Now he had heard.

Again, the drowsy scent of Hannah's cooking warmed the air. When Goldman straightened, the weight in his spine and shoulders shifted painfully. He was bone-tired. But he dug his elbows on the table and began re-reading the letter, for the third time. Twelve pages, neatly pinned, and covered to the very edge with an urgent, exact hand. The paper itself was grey. It was emblazoned at the top: *Hotel de France*, Cracow, and the *w* ended in a baroque flourish which rejoined the crest of the *C*.

Even as he strained to keep his attention unwavering, to hold in abeyance the impulse of anger and blame, Goldman remembered Aaron's loud pleasure at the Polish stamps.

Dear Dr. Goldman,

Early on, you warned me against writing letters. A patient who writes his analyst is evading. I know. But this time it's different. I have to write because I won't be seeing you again. And I'm not running away. I'm coming clean. Now that's a queer one. One never *comes* clean. You know, in the other sense. Here am I starting to play the game, to find things *inside* words. It hasn't been a waste. I've learnt a lot from you. Don't think I'm ungrateful. Only ashamed. About that last bit.

Those were not *my* dreams. Not the last three weeks. I kept hoping you'd guess. Then I didn't want you to. I realized that it wasn't fair, that I was playing a nasty trick. But it is odd that you didn't smell a rat (I lost £100 betting that you *would*). Perhaps you did and weren't letting on. You said once that a patient can't lie, not really, because his lies are often the loudest part of the truth. So you listened, as if those dreams had been my own, and helped me spin the filth and cunning out of them. On the last day, I was damn near to telling you. But I couldn't face up to it. And it didn't seem to matter any more. Because those fake dreams made me see myself as I am. More than anything else that has ever happened to me, or that you've said. Now that I think of it, you never did say very much. I suppose that's the art of it. Make the patient scour the wall until it turns to a mirror. Make *him* do it, or he won't get a sharp look at himself. I have. Right inside those counterfeit dreams. After that, I knew whom I wanted to see before I packed up. That's why I left to come here.

Is that what Reeve wanted? He wrote those dreams out on small sheets of blue note-paper, and sent them twice a week, registered. I had promised to learn them by heart and try them on you. It makes my skin crawl to write this. I know what you'll think of me. I'm sorry. Please believe that. He said he would show you up for a fraud, so I would have to stand on my own feet. In a way, I'm sorry you didn't guess (I couldn't really afford that hundred quid). But I don't see that it proves anything about analysis. Either way. We don't close down the National Gallery just because it's bought a fake picture. And I don't think that's what Reeve was after. Not really. He hates the whole business, a man pouring his vomit into another man's lap. That's how he put it. I dare say there's something in that. Like a chap in the mess not able to keep down his liquor and puking all over his orderly. And Reeve got a dose of it in America. To listen to him, you'd think it was the national sport over there. But there was something *else*.

In the old days we were very close. I could tell the mood he was in by the sound of his step half-way down the stairs. He used to finish my sentences for me. We had words we shared with no one else. Reeve was faster than I, and much, much cleverer. But I had more weight. When the gale caught us, that time off the Broads, he said he'd pitch me overboard and use me for an anchor. But during the war we lost touch. And for me there was someone else. I don't know how to put this without making it sound crazy. But I wonder whether it was *you* Reeve was after, whether it was really the analysis that enraged him. He doesn't know about Jan. He couldn't. But a pointer will sniff a man and know if he's been with another dog. Reeve has a nose. He can smell the soul in you.

I didn't realize how alone he was when he came back from the States, how sick at the edges. I thought I needed him to keep those nightmares off. But they got worse. I must have been afraid that he'd get on to the scent, that he'd try and put his hand on something I wouldn't let him touch. Him or anyone. Not Sheila. Not you. So he went after it. Like a thief hunting for a hidden room in a house, tearing up the floorboards, making a shambles. Reeve lied about Ina. To keep me off balance, to make certain of my need. I don't have to lie to myself any more. Ever. She *was* going to have a child, and if I hadn't acted like vermin, if I'd gone to her and taken my chance, the whole of my life might have turned right.

But Reeve wouldn't have me free or out of his reach. He knew better than to worry about Sheila. It wasn't she who had stepped between us, who made him alone when we were together. I'm not saying he thought it all out, or planned it down to the last detail. I don't imagine that's how it happens. But the dreams he sent me were devilish clever. *You* must have known for a long time where the real trouble lay. But I wasn't going to admit it to myself. Reeve ground my face in the truth till it flayed my skin and nearly gouged my eyes out. He must have hoped that that would drive me back to him, that I would come all broken and reach out for him. We could hobble together, picking up the pieces of our lives, and stick close, close, as if there was only one wretched shadow for the two of us.

I know it sounds mad, but Reeve wanted the quick of me, the last secret place of the living spirit. So that he would never be alone, never again. That must be the sin they don't talk about, the one that can't be forgiven. To put your grip on another man's self, to filch it for your own use.

I promise you, I'm not off my head. I know that Reeve wouldn't understand half of what I'm saying (I can see the face he'd make reading this). But because of what's happened these last days, and because I know the end, I can look at things plain. As if an enormous cold light had switched on.

I imagine Reeve is pretty well damned for what he did, for trying to flush the soul out of me with those dreams. He'll walk the floors of hell blazing. And won't even feel it.

Not that it matters very much now. I've seen Jan, and that's what I have to tell you about. But first, there was the boy.

I had forty-eight hours' leave in Cairo. We knew there was a big push on. Every time I thought of what I was going back to, my insides did a flip. So I kept on the move, buying a lot of fancy trash and crowding it in a room, a hidden place of my own, in a jumble of mud-houses and garden down by the river. Carved fly-swatters, a stuffed cat with yellow glass eyes—Hamid swore by his mother's sacred tits that they were topaze—a Turkish musket, a grand thing all chased in silver. To make the room so absurdly and secretly my own, that I would have to come back to it, dead or alive.

On the second day, I did the bazaars. You have to dive deep holding your breath. The usual pack was at my heels, and all around me, feeling my clothes and shrilling. If you haven't seen it, the living filth and misery of wog children is something no one can make you believe. There were the things one reads about: the open sores, the worms they squeeze out of themselves in the street, the flies hanging in bunches from the mouths and eye-lids of the blind. But what I hadn't known about was that smell—a yellowish smell that came at you from their breath and skin—the smell of hunger. I took what change I had and bought a bagful of candied fruit, great sticky globbs. It was like tossing crumbs in the sea, gone in a minute, and the little devils pawing and whining at me worse than before.

Then the boy came. He was a head taller than the rest, and had marvellous white teeth. He kicked and flung about till the pack trailed off. Then he asked whether he could carry my purchases: "I shall not steal. By Allah, I shall not steal."

He walked just behind me, soft as a young wolf. It was hot; hotter than I'd ever known it, even in Cairo. More than likely, I had a touch of sun and fever. Everything around me seemed to flap. The fly-curtains, the awnings and tin shutters, the air like a stinking bat whirring and flapping around my head. We threaded our way home through those black alleys, the sewers running with filth. I thought I'd go mad if I didn't get to a cool place and a shower. I felt the boy at my heels. He had a high, dainty step, as if no dirt could touch him.

On a day like that, a room in which the shutters have been closed, or which gets a breath of wind off the river, is like a cold-box. I heard his teeth click as he put down the bird-cage—it had brass foliage and little bells, and must have been lifted from one of the old French whore-houses—and a cane I'd haggled for, with an ivory handle. He slipped around the room, looking at my gear, passing his hand over my towels and bed-sheets. The flapping was in my brain, and I was anxious to get rid of him. I dug in my pockets for a bill, when I saw him pick up my flashlight. It had a blue plastic finish and a switch to cut the beam high or low. You can get it at any Woolworth, but I could tell he'd never seen anything like it. He switched it on and played it against the wall. He was so excited that he'd stopped breathing.

"I want this. Please give it to me. Please, gracious Sir."

"Why should I? What will you do for it?" I meant nothing saying it.

"I'll do anything, Effendi, anything."

It was the word *anything*. It must have unhinged me; I could hear the nerves inside me going strange. I don't think I uttered a word. But he looked at me grinning. He was only wearing shorts and a rag around his neck. When I put my forehead against his naked skin, it was all burning and cool. Then I must have lost control. I turned him around and pushed him on to the bed. Even if I wanted to, I couldn't tell you what happened. I don't remember. Only his laugh when he slid out the door.

After a while, I came around and saw he had taken the flashlight, my plastic raincoat, a pack of Player's and two tins of dried milk.

When I was a child and had been wicked—"played with myself" or cribbed—I was sure I'd perish the next day, in some hideous accident. Unless I could do certain laborious magic rites, hammer my head against the floor when saying my prayers, or flip a knife into the ground off the back of my hand, nine times in a row. Even then, I knew something would go wrong, that I'd be punished.

After the boy, I expected that I'd be killed the moment I got back in the show. I even wrote the usual letter: "To be sent in case of . . ." I was literally waiting for the bullet to plough through me. Actually, it was a piece of shrapnel, two nights later, on a forward patrol near Sidi Meraa. I remember lying there wondering why it took so long to die, and why it didn't hurt more. I tried to think of the boy, and found I couldn't remember his face. Then they picked me up.

The base hospital was overcrowded and there were holes in the fly-netting. That can be torture, with the sand-flies going at your bandages and the heat coming down on you like a foul blanket. There wasn't enough of anything to go around except English ladies from Cairo, elderly ladies mostly, with cool dresses, asking whether they could write letters for you or read to you from the Good Book. Most of the chaps were browned

189

off, and made fun of them behind their backs. But I thought them rather sporting, and so did Jan.

He was in the bed next to mine. He had a Polish accent and courtly manners. When one of the old girls had read to him, he would stick his head out from under the netting and kiss her hand, saying "Thank you, Madam, I am your debtor." The other men found it a huge joke. But Jan had a trick of staring you down. His eyes were night-blue; I'd never seen anything like them. He had pitch-black hair, and despite the desert his skin had stayed pale. He was small, but all wire. The rest of us shuffled in those shapeless grey slippers they handed out; he moved down the ward like a fencer, his heel barely touching.

The medical chaps were a bit afraid of him. When he said, "I shall be out of here in ten days from *now*, and I want no misunderstanding about that," they smiled feebly and went to the next bed. Soon he announced to Matron, in a tone of implacable sweetness, that there were only four days to go. Would she be so gracious as to see that his kit was ready. She tried her bark, but before she could get a sentence out, Jan had bounded from his cot, bowed low, and proffered a small bouquet of violets (God knows how or where he had managed to get them; they were dark as velvet). The old sea-cow burbled into complete submission: "Oh, Lieutenant Jan. Oh." No one ever tried his full name.

He served as liaison between our brigade and the Second Polish Army. His motor-cycle had triggered a mine. The driver was blown to shreds, but the sidecar came down on top of Jan and he had only flesh-wounds.

He had seen his family—his father, mother, and two sisters, one aged twelve—herded into a barn by the SS. Then they had set the barn alight. Cowering under a pile of dung and wet leaves, Jan had watched the flames and heard the screams in the fire. Somehow, he had escaped and got across the Baltic. The Danes put him in a foster home. It was a barrack and smelt of tar-soap. When the Germans came, he smuggled his way on to a herring trawler. They were blown off course and had no water to drink the last forty-eight hours. They reached harbour, somewhere in East Anglia, and the authorities were gravely perturbed because Jan had no papers. He still laughed under his breath when he recalled their embarrassed mien, or how they'd said "There'll be tea served in a moment," when he asked for water.

At eighteen, he had joined the Polish forces in London. Now he was in the desert, "running errands and killing Germans." He was the first man I met who thought of it in that way, who had a personal war. He said that whenever he could, he shot low, so that they would feel themselves die. Once he had surprised a three-man German patrol dead-asleep near their weapons-carrier. He stole in barefoot and slit the throats of two of them, leaving the poor bugger in the middle to wake between them. "I don't want to survive this war, Maune. It would be a jolly bad thing if I did. They'd have to put me in a cage." But mostly he spoke of books or music. And when the pains came on (I had a splinter of the bloody thing in my kidney), Jan would bend over from his cot, hold my wrist, and whistle like a thrush.

We took our convalescent leave together. Jan bought a victrola with a large, antique horn, and set it in the midst of my loot. He rifled the bazaar of old records. I had never known much about music. It wasn't the sort of thing you did at school. Now we lay in the dark listening, Italian opera mostly, and those hot, cracked voices pouring out gusts of life. The cicadas in the garden rose to the sound. Often we were too lazy or entranced to get up; the record went on hissing under the needle, and behind it came the wailings from the river. There was one tune Jan played over and over. I don't suppose I've got the name right. *Nessun dorma:* "No one sleeps in the city tonight." And the voice made a wild, soaring curve. We didn't sleep either. It was too hot; the air was so heavy you could push it with your hand. And there was so little time. Our chit only ran to a week.

It's the only time in my life I've been completely happy. At peace. He liked to lie on the floor, his blue eyes open, like embers. Watching Jan, I knew what it meant to be in love with another human being. To say anything you wanted, even if it was new or confused, without having to talk. As if one's body, and the mere fact of being near, had voice. It sounds like pretentious rubbish, and I don't imagine I can make you see it. I've told you how close I was to Reeve, and I've been fond of Sheila. More than that. I've loved her in my own way, and wanted her. It's excited me to know she was in the house, to hear her moving about. But when I compare that to what I felt for Jan, it's as if I was talking another language. It's the only time I've stopped being *me*, that I've got out! Skin, my castle, my cell. But not with Jan. As if you could melt into another person, not to pillage, not to master, but to lie at rest in.

I thought we would both be killed soon. That made it all clear and right. It was the marvellous trick death had in store. The schedule had gone awry and we were being allowed a taste of it while we were still in the sun, and could hear each other turn in sleep.

I told him about the boy. Jan made a flute of his cupped hands and blew a long note, like the blind man in the café. Then he laughed and said that the English were voluptuaries of remorse. He repeated it in Polish and it came out like dry wood cracking. He believed there was *no* experience one should forgo, not with death our neighbour. He was certain that the soul was immortal only through the power of its memories, that the strong grass over graves came from recollections thrown like seed into the rushing dark. One must not go empty-handed, but with such store of particular remembrance that eternity would seem too hasty. It was not Plato or Aquinas had proved the soul immortal, but Proust. I had never heard of Proust. Jan drummed on the wall and said I was a barbarian. And a hypocrite; for having bribed the boy: "Love bought is like old fish. It leaves a smell."

You remember that time I flew into a black rage. Because you were making me out to be a queer. I wouldn't have it. Not then, or at any time. This was something else. Utterly. I suppose I lied to you when I said Jan and I had not touched. But not really. The lie is in you and in anyone stupid enough to think that the words meant anything of what happened between us, that they tell even an inch of the truth. The words are beastly. And meaningless. As if you were trying to make a man see the sun by the dark of its leaving.

I've known something—I dare say it was only a minute—which most human beings—oh, the lot of them—never get a glimpse of, not in their wildest dreams. We touched. Hardly that. Mostly, we only lay near each other. But I can swear by God's face that the stuff in the poems is true, about the stars coming down on top of a living man. I know because it happened. In that room—and the blackness outside holding its breath, going dead still.

I won't re-read this letter. I'd be afraid to. It must sound like drivel. But why should I care? I'd cry it from the rooftops if I could. This *has* happened to me. I've heard my own soul dance. If you don't believe me, it's because it's never happened to you. Don't you see? I've had all the luck.

And am doomed for it, I suppose. Because I've gone around comparing everything else in my life to that week—to those two or three nights out of time. It's made all the rest ash in my mouth.

I tried to forget about it. You know how hard I tried, all the games I played with myself. But just as Jan said, forgetting is the death of you. The real living death. You walk about and act as if you're alive, but you're stone dead inside. I was honest about Sheila. I pitched my heart into it. But it was never as good. Not like that bit of flame. Right in the marrow.

That's the whole truth. I'm not going to try and tell you any

193

more. I'm rich. I'm taking it with me. You can close your file (how I hated that brown cover!) and put at the end: *repressed homosexual*. I don't care, because it's gibberish. Like a monkey spewing words. It means nothing. Not to *me*.

Perhaps it would to Jan. Perhaps it would put him in a fury. I don't know. Because he's different now. I had to go and see him once more. After Reeve tried to cheat the living daylight out of me. I had to see Jan, to make sure that he remembered, that there was someone else in the world who knew the truth, who could tell me that I hadn't dreamt miracles. I *have* seen him. These last few days. As I say, he's different.

I could tell the moment I saw him. He sat encased in a square-cut tunic, and a great laugh was coming out of him, raucous, out of the belly. He rose at me, arms flung wide, calling my name, but not looking at me, not straight. We hugged and panted at each other like circus bears. He had told me to meet him in a kind of tavern, in the Old City, down a flight of stone steps. They're rebuilding that part of Warsaw, brick by brick, to get it exactly as it was, the same doorknockers, the same window-boxes. To prove you can't make oblivion, even with dynamite, and so memories will have a place to lean on. Rather like what you're doing, isn't it? Brick by brick. Clearing the rubble with a fine-tooth comb.

There was a mob, but Jan barged through. Two women were sitting at our table. They flurried about me, kissed me, and dabbed their faces. One was his wife, the other her cousin or best friend. I couldn't make it out. They spoke very little English and kept saying my name as if they had a sweet at the end of their tongues. Jan shouted for the waiter, and we drank a gulp of something that went down like raw flame. It nearly spun me out of my chair, but the women pounded my back and said "Hallo Gerald, hallo Gerald." My eyes were tearing and Jan looked bulky and far away. They heaped our table with small dishes, all hot and full of seed, and paraded around us carrying burning things on spits. The other woman—a tall girl

194

with flat shoulders and pale, sandy hair—kept putting little dabs and bites on her spoon and passing them to me. I didn't know what I was eating. It made me steamy inside, so I poured that iced blazing stuff down my throat. Each time we emptied a bottle, they stuck a candle in it, and soon there was a lit crown in the middle. I could see Jan's face through a hot mist; it ran sweat.

We danced. There were so many people packed in that stifling cellar, that all you had to do was clutch tight and turn on your heels. The girl pressed her hands in the small of my back, and I could taste the wine on her breath. Jan kept lurching into us, or giving me a happy jab with his boot. I don't suppose they've seen many Englishmen in Warsaw, and Jan sang out at the top of his voice about how we'd fought together in the desert and eaten Jerries alive. So men and women crowded close, perfect strangers, all gaping and excited, carrying fruit-brandy or vodka, and demanding that I drink with them. Then the band played *Tipperary* (would you believe it? *Tipperary*—in this day and age!), and the girl laid her cheek to mine. It was full of tears.

We slogged our way back to the table. It was again heaped with food and sweet wine. As we sat down, the girl caught my hand and set it on her knee. My head was hammering, and I could see the whole room taking a slow turn. But I felt her running my palm up and down her stocking, all the way under her dress, right to the skin. When I drew away, she swayed after me and drooped her head on my shoulder. Jan and his wife winked and made noises, like children at a party. Then the two women went off to the powder-room, their arms around each other.

Jan and I locked elbows and drank, the way he'd taught me in Cairo. He said I looked puffy and out of sorts—"like salt haddock." Poland would put life in me. Yes, he'd stayed in the army. Killing was the only thing he'd ever been trained for properly. He was too dangerous to be let out of the zoo. So he was in the cage, but at the lion's end. He was a colonel now.

Colonel Jan. I tried to ask more, but he cut me off. "No serious talk tonight." There'd be plenty of time for that. I ducked and some of the brandy dribbled on to my collar, but Jan got it down me anyway, and the women were back saying we should dance.

The fiddles came at us and the band tapped their red lacquered boots on the floor. I was in the middle and felt the girl's hold go soft and spin away. People were clapping hands and shouting at me to do a reel. I must have looked a damned fool. But the clapping came quicker and quicker, as if blackbirds were at my head, and I could hear glass breaking. Then the ceiling took a sickening dive and I shut my eyes.

Jan caught me and trotted me up the stairs in a rush. We were in a black, wet yard. The air was ice. It belted me in the stomach and I threw up. Jan held my head, laughing: "You're out of practice, Gerald! You remember the night at the mess, when you made me drink Black Velvet till it came out of my ears!" I cleaned up in the washroom and tried to drink from the tap. It came out rusty, and Jan brought a bottle of mineral water. I felt better, just a little chill and light in the head. Jan was telling me about the girl. Her fiancé had been shot down in the rising. Two Russians had found her crouching in a sewer. They'd taken their time with her. Now she had a taste for men. But she was a fine girl and would show me the sights. I wanted to find out about Jan's wife, about what he'd been up to. But he talked in a loud, flailing torrent, and I couldn't stop him.

It must have been three in the morning before we shambled out of the place and into Jan's jeep. There are few cars in Warsaw and he's madly proud of his. The girl and I bundled in the back seat and he yelled at us to hold tight. He made wild, clucking sounds at the ignition as if it was a horse. Then he jammed the accelerator to the floor and we swung out of the cobbled square in a screech. There are hardly any lights, and the roads are makeshift tracks between craters and piles of rubble. Suddenly you're in a maze of high walls, with window-frames hanging loose, or bits of bath-tub swaying in the empty air, then back in the charred waste, up to the mud-guards in yellow water.

Jan whipped the car in and out of those smashed streets as if we had been on the Le Mans circuit. We were shouting, but when he turned or slammed the brakes, it knocked the wind out of us. All the time, he was damning or coaxing the jeep in a high-pitched call.

We careened through a foul pit, with an old coil of barbed wire lashing the wheel, and over a mound of debris on the other side, when the whistles started behind us. Jan pulled the jeep to a sudden halt; the girl fell all over me, gasping. Jan grinned at us like a small, devilish boy: "That'll be the militia. They hate the army, and they hate anyone who can run their own car. They've got a little Russian job. Pure junk. I can beat them blindfold. And they know it. Now watch!"

He caressed the wheel and we ripped away. Down a tunnel of broken walls and mudholes. There were no street lamps and Jan kept his own lights low. Shadows and solid edges flew at us, and I kept my head down in complete panic. The whistles were closing in, and I could hear Jan sing between his teeth. The militia had us in their headlights when he threw the jeep into a mad turn, two wheels off the ground, shot over a wooden trestle, and through a gate into sudden calm. The militiamen whistled and shouted, but had stopped outside. Jan tilted his head back and let out a happy roar: "Military zone! Off bounds. They can't follow us here. It's about the only place where the weasels can't get at you." I made out a dim hulk of barracks and saw a sentinel—he wasn't more than a boy—give a startled salute.

The women sat up and rubbed the jolt out of their ribs. Their breath came short and excited. Jan said he and his wife had a fine room in the officers' compound. That was a feat. Rooms were hard to come by. Why didn't we go up now and get a bit of sleep, the four of us. The girl gave a tense giggle and pressed against my thigh. Jan said there was room to spare. We would make coffee—real coffee—and get out of our clothes. He too was excited and looked straight into the dark.

I said No; that I'd rather go back to my hotel and meet him the next day. He turned and gave me an odd stare. Then he explained to the two women, with heavy gaiety, that in England it was customary for ladies and gentlemen to separate after dinner. *Ladies* and *gentlemen*; he repeated the words with hollow emphasis. We shook hands and embraced, and the two women trailed off across open ground. I climbed into the front seat and Jan started the motor.

He drove carefully now, without pleasure. We crossed a moon landscape of ruin, and came to the edge of the river. Jan halted. We watched the first streak of dawn stain the high bluffs on the eastern bank.

"That's where the Red Army stood and waited during the rising. They didn't even let their artillery open fire on the Germans. We sent couriers swimming across, desperate for help. But they waited. Till the *Wehrmacht* had wiped us out and killed the best."

He said it without hate or insurgence, nearly in admiration of a tactic so far-reaching, so tenacious in nerveless cunning.

"What they liberated was a desert full of women and starved children. The women were so shell-shocked that many of them didn't utter a sound when the Kazahks grabbed them. But now Ivan's our ally, and we get to love him better each time you ship a tank or gun to Adenauer. What fools you are. To trust Germans. To buy the tiger a new set of teeth."

Light was beginning to move on the water. I told Jan I had not come to argue politics, but to talk about the past, about the strong remembrance that kept us from the dark. What had happened to our room in Cairo? Who used it now? And did Jan remember the elephant-foot umbrella stand? I had to make sure that my poor devil of a soul hadn't fed on lies.

He lit a cigarette and blew a smoke-ring, and watched it unwreathe in the cold air.

"What is there to talk about? Does it worry you? It's something that happens to boys, in the school lavatory, or when they're out together in the woods. In the green woods. We were both a little slow growing up. That's all. Why churn up your guts about it?"

I cried out. His voice was like pain inside me. He couldn't mean what he'd just said. It was too stupid, too vulgar. It left me nothing.

Jan heard. I knew because the lines of his face had gone sharp. But he wasn't listening.

Instead: "Why were you so awkward back there? Acting like a wet hen. You should have gone with us. That's a nice girl. You've hurt her feelings."

I couldn't get the words right. Like treacle in my mouth. But I tried. God, how I tried! To make him see why I'd come. How it was the world to me. I tried to tell him about Reeve and those dreams. About the voices in the fire (I know *now* whose voices they were). How they burnt and hammered in my skull. I won't repeat to you what I said. I couldn't bear to. I was skinning myself alive. Right there sitting in that car. Every layer of me. Till I could smell myself, down deep. I swear to you it made me sick.

And all the time he was smoking and looking at the river. No one could have stood it long without going wild. To be so alone right next to him, to cry into the wind and get nothing back. It was God awful. He just sat there, all blank and armoured, and kept his sleeve from brushing against mine.

He let me talk until my mouth went dry. Then he turned the ignition and looked straight at me. It was the first time that night.

"Ah, you English. You voluptuaries of remorse."

He didn't remember that he had said it before. I know he didn't remember. But because the words were the same, exactly, because they came out with that same cracked sound, time went weird. For a moment we were back in our room in Cairo. I swear we were. Jan's eyes had that hot, blue point in them. It made me go soft and a bit crazy with remembrance. I must have leaned towards him or looked out of hand. Because he hit me, oh not hard, but enough to knock me out.

I woke in my hotel room, sick as a dog. I sat on my bed retching, and felt so sorry for myself I bawled.

After a while, I found Jan's note. He had torn a page from my diary where it had fallen on the floor when he carried me in.

He said we had drunk too much. We were old men now and shouldn't have got so pissed. He was sorry. He didn't really remember the things I had referred to. In any case, he was sure they weren't worth raking up. He couldn't imagine life without Rada, and hoped that I too would soon get married. He misspelt *married*.

That's all there is to tell. I left for Cracow the next morning. To be some place else. This is a handsome town, and I've had time to get things untangled.

I don't care about anything any more. Or *anyone*. That's the best time to decamp, isn't it?

I'm sorry about all the trouble, and about lying to you. But that's under the bridge now. I know you'll give Sheila what help you can. She's a level-headed girl, and she'll be all right. Life owes her another turn. I'd like to have told Reeve that he was too clever by half. Right to his hound's face. And to see the ash on him. Because he's going to burn. Believe me. He's going to burn.

But it doesn't matter now. Nothing does. It's a queer, grand feeling, like the time I flopped into the Dead Sea and it carried me so easy I could sleep on the water.

I imagine this is quite the longest letter you've ever had. I feel rather posh taking it to the post-office. But I'd best get on with it.

Wars kill a long time after, don't they? Thanks for everything.
Yours very sincerely,
GERALD MAUNE.

For a long time, Goldman kept staring at the neatly pinned bundle of paper, helpless. As soon as he had read the letter, he had alerted Mrs. Maune and Reeve, and cabled the embassy in Warsaw.

Now he was waiting for news. But not really. Simply for the ring of the bell or the voice at the door which would confirm what he knew already. A man does not need to draw the curtain when it has been snowing the night through, he hears the dead quiet in the morning air.

Goldman rubbed his palms against the blotter. They were numb. A mortal tiredness bent him. In a corner of his mind he was aware that Hannah had called to dinner, that she had knocked twice at the door of his study. But moments passed before he could turn his head and answer.

9

Gerald Maune left the post office feeling beautifully easy. It was a mood he could place. The last Friday of term, in the afternoon, when the trunks stood ready and the clothes boxes tightly roped, when the sheets had been stripped from the beds, leaving only the neat square of blankets. There were always twenty minutes or half an hour in hand before the bus loaded, taking the boys to the station and the start of the journey home. Gerald would stroll in the garden, by the long wall, and watch Brackens go silent, the cries and rush of feet passing from it, like a covey of loud birds receding.

After the rubble and crude renascence of Warsaw, Cracow intact was balm. Gerald set out for the castle, but was soon enmeshed in a hive of cobbled streets. The contour of bastions and turrets, which rode high over the city, had vanished behind the near gables and chimney-pots. He sought to retrace his steps and looked up at the street-signs with their spiky consonants, so many dragons mute. A girl stopped and asked whether she could be of help. Her English was brave but short of breath. She had plain, broad features and wore glasses. In her brown mackintosh and cork-soled shoes, she looked old and a little charred. She said she was an art-student and would be happy to show him the way. She didn't have much chance to practise her English. Again, Gerald was struck by a quickness of encounter he had found everywhere in these last few days, as if the crowd of the dead—you caught the dry whisper of their feet even here, in the unbroken streets—had drawn the living close.

They leaned over the parapet in a blaze of sky, watching the river swing its loop around the city. Then she showed him the baroque palais, the improbable pleasure house of cream and gold, carved by Italian craftsmen, far from home, into the glooms of the citadel. There was a ramp broad enough for horsemen to ascend and enter the dining-hall mounted. Gerald strode up it and the girl looked after him, smiling. They threaded their way down bent lanes and worn flights of stairs, to the market square and the Trumpeter's Tower.

Gerald asked the girl to have tea with him. She peered at her watch, tugged the sleeve back over her wrist, and said she would be pleased. The small pastry shop was crowded with people who had a harried air but seemed in no particular haste. They found a corner of a table and Gerald brought a plate of cakes. They tasted of chalk, faintly sweetened. The girl made apologetic motions. It was all very difficult. Too many people swarming into the towns, and grain being left to mildew because there were not the lorries to carry it or the bins to store it in. But tea came in a steaming glass and Gerald said it tasted fine.

She was writing a doctoral dissertation on "Botticelli and his use of Medieval Motifs". Had Gerald been to Italy?

He told her he had had his fill of it during the war.

She asked about the Mantegnas and the Medici chapel. Had he seen Urbino and St. Ambrose in Milan?

Gerald ransacked his memory for details of pictures vaguely wondered at, of basilicas hurried past in the tumult and boredom of troop movements. As he spoke, the focus sharpened, and he found himself hauling to the light clear-edged shards of knowledge, fragments crystallized into bright certainty, and far more vivid than he thought he possessed. She drew him on hungrily, and he recounted a visit to Torcello, in a captured German barge, smoke still hanging on the brackish waste of the lagoon. The island stood unkempt, the grass rank, and burnt or bloated things drifted between the rotted palings. He had climbed the *campanile*, as up a tower of silence, and looked back on the silhouette of Venice, bone-white on the winter sea.

The girl was crying, with loud sniffles. Gerald flushed, but no one else seemed to take notice. She apologized, blowing her nose and wiping her glasses against the hem of her dress. She had read of all these marvels, ah interminably, seeking the strong light of their wonder on the dead page or browned photograph. She had told the rosary of their names—Volterra, San Gimigniano, Masaccio—till the beads had worn lucent in her mind. Now she was lavishing heartache and years—years unrecapturable and that would leave her dry—trying to write of the strange master and his shapes of flame. But she would never see those towers or *piazzas*; never pass her fingers over the living stone. "I am a blind man gossiping about colours!"

But why? Why should she not go?

She blew her nose again and tried to smile at the innocence of Gerald's challenge. It came from another world. Very few were allowed to travel. And then, only the scientists.

Things would change. They were improving all the time.

Not for her. She had not been adroit about "politics and such matters". She had cried out of envy, out of naked desire. Because Gerald was so unutterably free. To go where he pleased. Because he could see Aracoeli again, on its high throne of stairs.

Gerald said he didn't think he would do much travelling

after this. In the west, too, there were bends and sharp corners for the heart to bruise against.

She pressed her hand on his arm; she didn't want to hear about those. It would only make it more difficult.

Gerald saw an ink-stain on her fingers and felt a keen impulse to rub it off, to grasp her ungainly, chafed hand in his. But that would have meant a temptation of disorder, a crease in the blanket, so he smoothed the thought away.

Outside the tea-shop, he said that he was sorry he had upset her. It was stupid of him. But she bent close with denial, and her face shone. He had made her very happy. She would remember everything he had told her, every detail. Did he know how lucky he was? And as she walked away, still pressing her wet handkerchief, she turned and waved.

Gerald went back to his hotel and asked for the bill. He explained that he might be leaving very early the next morning. The clerk demurred. There was no early train to Warsaw, and he added, piqued, that there would always be someone at the desk. Monsieur was in a first class hotel. Gerald insisted. The clerk took the money with displeasure and muttered dimly that there might be extras at breakfast. If Monsieur had eggs. A flash of rage passed through Gerald, a desire to cry out the titles and ceremonies of death. But he checked himself and went quickly to his room.

Looking for the bottle of pills, small mauve capsules under a tuft of cotton, he found a clean shirt, the laundry-wrapper still on it. It filled him with a sense of waste, of means unspent or sown to the wind. He wanted to take out the pins, to wear the shirt and soil it in some abrupt extravagance of gesture. Then he laid it back in his travelling-case, and said out loud, not knowing why, "To the church of the Laodiceans, To the church of the Laodiceans," twice.

A little later, he started out of a cold, dragging sleep. Through the glass of the bottle, now empty, he could see the window. It had been wrenched open and the sky was spilling into the room. He was choking under its bright, towering mass and wondered, brokenly, how air could strangle. He knew that he must reach the window and close it fast against the racing tide.

Gerald Maune tried to get to his feet. But suddenly there was no need. A perfect stillness was in the room, and when he held out his hand, he touched it.